MURDER ON THE CORAL QUEEN

(A Dr. Gwen Gordon Mystery)

by

J. H. Russo

Copyright © 2008 by J. H. Russo

ISBN 0-7414-4971-4

Published by:

INFINITY
PUBLISHING.COM

1094 New DeHaven Street, Suite 100
West Conshohocken, PA 19428-2713
Info@buybooksontheweb.com
www.buybooksontheweb.com
Toll-free (877) BUY BOOK
Local Phone (610) 941-9999
Fax (610) 941-9959

Printed in the United States of America

Printed on Recycled Paper

Published September 2008

To Donna & Frank
Enjoy
John Russo

Books by John Russo:

The Bennie Arnoldo File

Indian Givers

The Vandenberg Diamonds

Dedicated to Jamie for inspiring
me to write this book

CHAPTER 1

New York

"What do you mean, I'm fired?" Herb Marshall, Senior VP of Silvers Cosmetics, erupted out of the red Italian leather chair he was seated in.

Yvonne Silvers, the sixty-three year old owner of Silvers Cosmetics, sat cold-faced as his words resounded within the expansive posh office she considered her throne room.

Silvers Cosmetics was located in the Crawford Building on Lexington Avenue between Forty-sixth and Forty-seventh Streets. Her office, along with the offices of several other executives, was on the top floor of the two floors the company occupied. From there, Yvonne ruled with single-minded arrogance. She had no qualms about crushing anyone, especially subordinates, if and when she chose, for any infraction she felt was against herself or her company.

"That's right, you ingrate. Pack up your desk today," she snarled stroking her coifed hair as she rose and faced him. The afternoon sun streamed through the windows behind her desk creating an exaggerated silhouette of her large frame.

Herb squinted as her diamond teardrop earrings refracted the brightness. "Does Mel know you're doing this, Yvonne?" he stammered as he tried to control the fury he felt building inside him.

"You know that my husband is president in title only. He's merely a figurehead around here, just as you've been. Unfortunately, my company needs bodies to achieve my goals, and that's all you and the rest of those overpaid drones mean to me."

"I promise you'll come to regret this someday, Yvonne. And those drones, as you call them, are some of the best in our industry."

"Be that as it may, from now on they're not your concern. Now get out." She turned her back on him and faced Lexington Avenue.

Herb pushed over a chair and side table as he stormed out, slamming the hand-carved teak door behind him.

"Witch," he shouted back as he passed by her secretary's desk.

The poor girl had her head turned away from the shouting that had emanated from her boss's office. She silently mouthed the words, "I'm sorry, Mr. Marshall."

Herb stomped his way down the corridor lined with beauty shots of various models as he headed directly to Mel Silvers' office at the opposite end of the floor.

He actually reported to Mel, so it seemed only logical at this point to have the last word with him. He was well aware that Yvonne controlled Silvers, including its namesake Mel, but Herb had to get some satisfaction and a more reasonable explanation as to what had just happened to his career.

Mel's secretary, obviously aware of the commotion as Herb's door slamming resonated from one end of the corridor to the other, smiled meekly as he approached. He nodded in her direction and, without waiting for any response, barged in on Mel Silvers.

"Herb. What can I tell you…" Mel greeted him as soon as he strode into the room.

A small man with a pleasant smile engulfed by puffy cheeks, Mel almost disappeared behind a desk that seemed to be much too large for him. To Herb it always looked as though his clear, green eyes could barely peer over the assortment of sample jars, lipstick cases, mascara color cards and counter display pieces scattered across the surface of his desk that were constantly being evaluated as possible additions to the Silvers line.

"Jeez, Mel, can you tell me why after almost ten years she does this to me? You know I've helped build this company into the success it is today."

"First of all, Herb, relax. Please have a seat." Mel got up, closed the door and walked across to an ornate credenza. "I keep a little brandy if you'd care to…"

"That's not what I need right now, Mel." Herb slumped into a chair, adjusted his horn-rimmed glasses and rubbed the stub of his red goatee.

Mel poured a drink for himself and then sat next to Herb and took a sip. "I knew this would happen when you told us that Global Health and Beauty Corp. had approached you…"

"For heaven's sake, Mel, you know what our industry's like. They were just putting out some feelers. Jeez, the only reason I mentioned it was so you and Yvonne wouldn't get wind of it along the grapevine. Besides, I wasn't interested in leaving Silvers, as you well know." He paused. "I'd better have that drink after all." Without waiting for Mel, Herb got up and helped himself at the credenza.

"I know all that," Mel said as he watched his private stock being poured into a Lalique crystal snifter. "But she heard it from who knows who and right away assumed that you were going to use their offer as a way of forcing her to increase your salary and bonus. I don't have to tell you how Ebenezer-like she is about executive compensation."

"Boy, do I know that. In spite of her attitude, my people and I have busted our humps for this company and earn every penny you pay us. This year our sales are bigger than her ego, and she has the nerve to pull this on me."

Herb watched as Mel took another swig and then realized there wasn't a thing this poor sap could do to improve his own situation let alone give him any solace. And worse yet, poor Mel was married to the witch.

"I'm sorry Herb, there's nothing I can do. If you decide not to go with Global, I'll personally give you the highest of references. I assume you'd rather tell your people?"

"I will, and thanks, Mel. And you can be sure Yvonne hasn't heard the last of Herb Marshall.

CHAPTER 2

Herb's Office

VP of Sales Bill Collin, VP of Marketing Barry Miller, and VP of Merchandising Jean Dawson had been summoned to Herb Marshall's office for the last time. They were seated around his oval conference table and he sensed by their expressions and fidgeting that they already knew what had happened.

A few moments later VP of R&D George Porter and Creative VP Simon Dumont straggled in and joined their teammates.

"Thanks for attending on such short notice," Herb began. "I know you're all up to your ears with the Honey Pot launch, but I'm sure you've all heard by now, knowing how thin these walls can be, that she finally did it. Yvonne picked up from somewhere that Global Health and Beauty was talking to me and that's all she needed to can me. Like I told Mel, I had one meeting with them and she assumed wrongly that I would use the opportunity to demand more compensation. I had no plans to even consider their offer until now, that is, and believe me, Yvonne will regret today."

With nothing further to add, Herb gazed fondly at the group that he had worked so closely with. It hadn't been all glitter and glamour, working for a serpent like Yvonne. He had often felt thankful for Mel who had been a buffer between him and Yvonne on important issues. Achieving success within the cosmetic industry was always a formidable task, not only was it a fierce competitive challenge but the wrong shade of lipstick or nail color could mean millions in lost sales affecting a corporation's bottom line and also their solid standing with the retail trade. As one market analyst had put it in a recent trade journal, "Selling cosmetics is nothing more than selling a promise, mostly smoke and mirrors."

For once Bill Collin had nothing humorous to say, "We're as shocked and upset as you are, Herb. She had no right to…"

"She has every right," George Porter declared from around the pipe he had clenched firmly between his teeth. "It's her fool company and we all know that, especially Herb."

"For once we agree on something, George," Herb replied.

Jean Dawson got out of her chair and went over to Herb. "We're going to miss you, Herb." She threw her arms around his shoulders. It was the first time Herb had ever seen her let down her strong competitive guard and display any feminine emotion. He was truly touched by the gesture. When she released him, she sheepishly said to the group, "Well, he's the best boss I've ever had." Shaking her shoulder-length hair, she returned to her seat.

Barry Miller, sitting as erect as usual, lit a smoke, paused, then spoke. "As crass as this sounds, Herb, who's going to approve all the marketing launch plans my department has worked on for the past several weeks? I mean, I've always depended on your support and Mel's to get things through her highness." He crushed out his cigarette after a few puffs.

"Come on, Barry," Simon interjected. "You're an ex-marine. You can handle her. She isn't as bad as some of the stuff you went through on Iwo Jima."

"Not amusing, Simon, and remember, you haven't gotten your Honey Pot print ads or the jar design approved yet," Barry snapped back.

"I guess what we're all really wondering, Herb, is who's our next COO?" George Porter put it to him bluntly.

Herb could see the sudden spark of interest on their faces that George's question induced. "I wasn't asked for a recommendation, nor did I offer one. Look, you all know it wouldn't have mattered anyway given the circumstances I'm leaving under."

"You mean Mel had no comment one way or the other?" Jean spoke up.

Simon looked up from a sketch he was doodling. "Come on, Jean, even if Mel had an opinion about that, she'd ignore him."

Herb could sense that this was turning into something other than his own frustration. "If it helps at all, my feeling is that anyone of you is qualified, so until the witch makes a decision, just do your jobs and keep quiet about your feelings toward me."

"That's going to be hard to do, Herb, given how well you've treated us," Bill Collin offered.

They all nodded their concurrence, even George Porter, who occasionally had disagreements with Herb over the potential commercial viability of R&D formulas Porter's lab had developed.

"Thanks for all your years of loyal and creative support. You've always made me look good, and if you ever need my help, look me up at Global." Herb stood as a sign the meeting was over.

As they filed out of his office, handshaking and one huge hug wrapped up the session.

CHAPTER 3

Silvers Conference Room

All five VPs were gathered in the Silvers' conference room. It was the week after Herb had been fired and their first status meeting with Yvonne and Mel.

"This is going to be one heck of a meeting without Herb as our mediator," Barry Miller noted. He studied his associates as he leaned back in one of the velour chairs surrounding the conference table.

Jean Dawson poured a glass of fresh squeezed orange juice from a serving credenza set up at the end of the room. "As true as that may be," she replied to Barry's comment before taking a sip, "Mel will certainly be more pro-active in Herb's absence."

"You've got to be kidding, Jean," Simon quipped as he opened his laptop. "Mel's like the rest of us, only he's married to the boss."

George Porter struck a match and fired up his pipe, took his seat, and then calmly predicted, "You're all overreacting. They have no choice but to approve the entire launch program. We've already refined it twice for Yvonne and she knows we're on a no-fault timetable."

"He's right," Bill Collin agreed nervously. "I've got my sales group geared up for the launch date and the last thing we need is to reschedule our client sales presentations. You have no idea how that would affect getting orders in before the holidays."

Barry watched as Bill, who was about to get a cup of coffee, quickly returned to his seat when the conference room door swung open.

*   *   *

Mel entered and headed for his usual place at the end of the table "Yvonne will join us shortly. Are we all prepared? No loose ends from our last meeting? If I recall, Simon, you had the most revisions to make."

"I'm ready, Mel," Simon replied as he double-checked his presentation material on his laptop screen.

With Herb no longer their leader, George Porter simply replied, "I believe we're all ready, Mel."

"Good, good," he said softly, then went on, "I know this is a difficult time. It's our biggest new product launch yet and, with Herb no longer with us, you know I'll do everything I can..."

"Do what, Mel?" Yvonne shook them up by her silent entrance. Without waiting for his reply, she headed for her seat at the head of the table. "Coffee, please."

Barry Miller, seated nearest to the credenza, got up and obliged her.

"I was just explaining how important this launch is to all of us and..."

"Yes, yes, let's get on with it, shall we?" She took the cup that Barry handed her, placed it on the table, then opened an ostrich hide folder and referred to her notes. "If you recall, Mr. Dumont," she turned her attention to Simon, then took a sip of coffee. "We weren't at all pleased with the model you chose for our print ads. Is that correct?"

Simon plugged in the cable that connected his laptop to a small PowerPoint projector, hit the F7 keys to sync it, then looked up and said, "That's correct, Yvonne. However, as your Creative VP, you know I didn't fully agree."

Mel cringed at the thought of what might be the beginning of another tirade-loaded meeting.

"You've made your point, little man. Now show me something worthy of the Silvers name on my advertising."

Simon abruptly hit the page-up key showing a print ad. It was a color photo of a beautiful woman in a garden setting, holding a tube of Honey Pot Moisturizer as she applied a dab on her blemish-free cheek. Simon read aloud the sell copy and then waited.

"Thank you, Simon," Mel spoke first. "I think you've captured the natural aspect of the honey concept." He stared down the table hoping Yvonne would concur.

"I feel we have," Simon stated.

"Not quite," Yvonne snapped. "I like the girl, but… I'm not sure the background is right. It's a little too sweet."

"Too sweet?" Simon questioned indignantly.

"That's how I feel about it, and you know I have a great feeling for these things. Go back and shoot it again, this time with a simpler background," she insisted.

Much to everyone's surprise, Simon quickly hit the enter key and the next ad layout appeared on the screen as he sharply declared, "I did." This photo ad layout was the same woman but with a soft-focus, distant country field in the background.

"That's better, Frenchman. You see, if you take my critiques positively, your work improves. Let's see, who's next?" She checked her notes.

Mel could almost see the fumes of anger coming out of Simon's nostrils as he shut down the laptop and flopped back into his seat.

"Ah yes, Ms. Dawson." Yvonne looked toward her VP of Merchandising.

"Well, now that we have some decent ads, can I assume you won't botch them up too much as counter displays?"

"Yvonne!" Mel scolded.

"I'm sure with Simon's fine touch our displays will be the best on every department store counter," Jean replied.

"They better be at the high costs your function generates. So try to be a little more responsible when it comes to wasting my money."

"Merchandising isn't a waste in our industry, Yvonne, and I'm very aware of..."

"All right, all right... don't start frowning, young lady. It's not good for your Scandinavian complexion."

Jean looked toward Mel with fire in her eyes.

"You'll do fine, Jean, I'm sure." That was all the comfort he could offer.

The remainder of the meeting went the same way. Yvonne wasn't too pleased with George Porter's R&D formulas. She assaulted Barry Miller's marketing plans as being too ambiguous, and Bill Collin's initial sales forecasts as totally unacceptable.

After she adjourned the meeting, Mel remained behind with his five angry, frustrated executives.

George Porter was the first to unwind. "Mel, we've been through this enough times to know it will all come together, and I know I'm speaking for all of us when I say that as loyal as we are to you, when it's all finished, one of us better be Herb's replacement."

None of the others spoke up, but from the determined looks he read on their faces as they left, Mel got the message.

*   *   *

As he sat alone in the quiet conference room, Mel reflected on that day almost ten years ago when he had interviewed Herb Marshall. The company had been growing faster than he and Yvonne had anticipated and, with Herb's background and experience with a small skin care company, Mel was certain he was the man to take Silvers into that profitable area of cosmetics. Of course, convincing Yvonne to hire Herb had been another matter. She hadn't much liked him when they met. She had said to Mel later that she didn't think he looked the part. "How can a short man with thick horn-rimmed glasses and a red goatee be knowledgeable in the world of cosmetics?" she had complained. But Mel had won her over and Herb Marshall had joined Silvers.

Yvonne had been easier to deal with back then in the days when he had been a buyer for Macy's and she had run their cosmetics department. He hadn't yet seen the change that was occurring. He had been impressed with her attractive elegance, and sharp mind the moment he met her. When he finally asked her out, she appeared cautious and inexperienced with men. Her shy nature seemed to blend with his soft demeanor. They had appeared to be the ideal match and, after a few months, she had accepted his proposal of marriage.

The shift in their relationship had started when Yvonne inherited a sizable amount of money from her father's estate. She had become possessive and unyielding with regard to her sudden wealth. It had caused a terrible rift between Yvonne and her only brother, Myron, and she had made it clear to Mel that he should stay out of her family affairs. Now here he sat in her company conference room, constantly belittled by her, not much more than a highly paid employee who lived with the sole owner of Silvers. Her only concession to him had been to name the company Silvers, and that was only because Rosen Cosmetics didn't have an upscale ring to it. Shaking his head and bringing his mind back to the current status of things, Mel got up, shut the lights and returned to his office.

CHAPTER 4

New York

It was well after six in the evening and most of the staff had left. Mel was standing behind Yvonne's desk staring down at the rush-hour traffic on Lexington Avenue. As usual, she was engrossed in some last-minute bit of business before they could leave for the day.

"You know, you couldn't have picked a worse time to let him go, Yvonne." He spoke still looking out at the city. Knowing she was ignoring him, he nonetheless continued to make his point. "Herb was key to our new Honey Pot launch and you completely disregarded that fact by once again losing control…"

That got her attention. She violently tossed a folder she was holding across her desk. "Don't you dare ever think for one minute that I'm not in control, Mel. Herb was disloyal, and I won't stand for that from anyone, not even you."

"You call this being in control?"

"That's about as useful as you are around here," she chided as Mel gathered up the scattered papers.

"That's enough, Yvonne," he cautioned as he placed the folder back on her desk. What's done is done, and I know you well enough to know that, although you won't admit it, you dumped him without concern for our launch or the company's balance sheet."

"You don't know me at all. Let's get out of here. I'm hungry."

*   *   *

The Chateau Moisson, two blocks from their Trump Tower apartment, was one of her favorite restaurants.

Over coffee, Mel broke into what had been almost a silent repast. Knowing she would behave reasonably in public, he spoke quietly, but firmly, "In light of the effect on morale that Herb's leaving will cause, I plan to do the following..."

"And what might that be, my compassionate husband?" She sneered but listened as he continued.

"I propose that rather than the loose-ends, pre-launch meeting at the Plaza that Herb had arranged, this time we do it in a more casual atmosphere."

"Perhaps you're actually starting to act like a president, Mel. So what is this morale pampering plan of yours?" she scoffed as she stirred her coffee.

"A cruise." He blurted out.

"You're joking." She wiped a drop of coffee from her lips as her mouth went agape in surprise. "A cruise instead of a Plaza meeting?"

"Yes, Yvonne. It came to me this afternoon. I checked with Bill Collin and he suggested the ideal cruise line. It seems they cater to small sales meetings and shipboard seminars."

"You and Bill Collin? Hah, you must have been at your office brandy..."

"Oh no you don't, Yvonne. Not this time." He could see she was uncomfortable being in a place where they were so well-known.

"Why should we expend resources on a cruise when a hotel meeting, and a fine one I might add, will do?" she replied with an artificial smile and a civil volume.

He had her where he wanted her, so he went full out. "Not only a meeting cruise, Yvonne, but with spouses included."

He could see her ire building and almost ready to erupt, so he concluded with a positive, "We're doing this, Yvonne, I'm having Bill set it up tomorrow and that's final."

He waited for the explosion he had weathered so many times before, but was shocked when she replied, "If you feel that strongly about it Mel, then I won't interfere."

Mel didn't know how to savor what he realized was his first victory in a long time as Yvonne signaled for their check.

It wasn't until later as they were preparing for bed that he realized he hadn't fully gotten the better of her after all when she announced, "Now that I think about it, Mel, this cruise idea of yours will work in more ways than one. It will, as you say, improve morale over Herb's departure, but should also lessen the blow as to who I plan to appoint to replace him."

"Who? What are you talking about?"

Mel was left without any explanation as Yvonne bid him goodnight and headed for her bathroom.

CHAPTER 5

Port Lauderdale
(Two weeks later)

"Here's George and Harriet now," Bill Collin called out as he rose to greet the Porters. They were all in the dining room of the Sandpiper Hotel in Fort Lauderdale. The Silvers group had arrived there the day before their cruise was scheduled to depart.

"Sorry we're late," George told the others.

"No problem," Collin replied. "We've all been enjoying some fine wine thanks to our expense accounts."

"And I'm sure we'll hear about it from her majesty when we turn them in," Jean Dawson held up her glass to greet the Porters.

"Allow me to reintroduce everyone," Barry Miller offered. "Harriet Porter, this is my wife, Helen." He then pointed around the table, "Simon's wife, Dina, Bill's wife, Marge, and Jean's husband, Jim."

They all nodded as he introduced them.

"Yes, of course, I remember you all," Harriet declared. "How could I forget after that terribly awkward outing Mel and Yvonne hosted out on the Hamptons?"

Jean whispered to Helen Miller seated next to her, "Who could forget the spectacle of those two egotistical women in the same room with each other. It was everything

Mel and George could do that day to keep them busy and apart."

"It wasn't all that bad, dear." George smiled and held out a chair for his wife.

"I'd like a very dry martini, George," Harriet said taking her seat next to Dina Dumont.

"And where are our illustrious leaders?" George asked as he signaled for the waiter.

"They're arriving in the morning and going directly to the ship," Barry answered.

"I'm looking forward to this little voyage," Jim Dawson told them. "I've never cruised before."

"You may never want to again after this one," Simon teased.

"We'd better all enjoy it," Collin cautioned. "Poor Mel went through a lot to talk Yvonne into this cruise."

"He does have our best interests at heart in spite of her," Jean added.

The waiter delivered Harriet's drink and stood by to take their dinner orders.

"Don't be in such a hurry, young man," Harriet spoke up after taking a gulp of her martini. "We just arrived and I need a little time to catch up."

George poured himself a glass of wine and said to the waiter, "Just bring my wife another martini, then we'll be ready to order dinner."

To break the tension while the rest of them waited for Harriet's need to be refueled, Bill Collin leaned forward as though he was about to divulge some national security secret and said, "You realize that besides our pre-launch meeting taking place on the high seas, I have a strong suspicion we'll each be evaluated as Herb's replacement."

"How do you know that?" Barry Miller questioned.

"Well, it would make sense," Simon agreed.

"Because," Barry explained, "when Mel gave me the go ahead to make the cruise arrangements, he kind of let it slip that Yvonne thought the casual setting would give her a chance to judge us more closely."

"It also means five days in the Caribbean with Yvonne," Simon stated.

"Yeah, so she can tear you all apart better," Harriet jumped in as she started on her second drink.

"I believe we're ready to order now, waiter," George quickly announced.

CHAPTER 6

The Coral Queen Pier 11

As they prepared to board the cruise ship Coral Queen, Harriet Porter nudged her husband, George, directing his attention to the printed greeting at the top of the gangplank.

'WELCOME SILVERS COSMETICS'

"At least they got that right," she complained.

For the past nine years George had been head of Silvers Research and Development and his latest creation, a honey-based complexion formula for wrinkles, Honey Pot Crème, would now make more millions for Silvers Cosmetics.

"I'm sure everything will be okay, Harriet. Collin arranged this trip and assured us that Sea Venture Lines was among the very best when it comes to accommodating groups likes ours. I understand that they even conduct computer seminars on these cruises."

Harriet raised the collar of her Versace jacket against the heavy fog as they waited halfway up the gangplank. "Well... they didn't get off to a very good start during check-in. It took forever to go through our luggage, and this photo they took for my ID card is out of focus."

"It's good enough for identity purposes on this cruise, Harriet, and that's all it's for. Look, mine's not much better." He held out his photo. "As for taking so long checking in, I suspected the pre-boarding scrutiny would be tedious. After all, security is a lot tighter these days. That's why I planned on an early start." He checked his watch.

"They could have at least provided refreshments in the security area. And now we're stuck in this fool line in the darn Fort Lauderdale morning dampness. Whoever heard of a cruise in March, anyway? I'm sure the Silverses chose the least expensive time of year. I'm not very happy, George, and put out that smelly pipe." She fanned the air in front of her nose. "You know how it annoys me."

"Sorry." He tapped out his briar, leaned down over her right shoulder and, drawing her close, replied softly, "Please try to be patient, dear. There're only a few people ahead of us. Once we're settled on board, I'm sure there'll be all sorts of refreshments."

But for Harriet's aggressive, complaining nature and her taste for martinis, George had always considered her the ideal wife for a cosmetics executive. As her youthful features were diminishing, she compensated for the loss by the heavy use of his products. Silvers Fiery Red hair coloring suited her short cut, Mellow Tangerine was the perfect shade to minimize her large lips, and Egyptian Night Eye Shadow completed the illusion of a fifty-year old woman reaching back for thirty. Harriet worked at her figure, and for that he was grateful. It was her best feature.

"It's about time," Harriet groaned. Their shipboard ID cards and cruise contracts were being checked by a tall chap in a neatly pressed white uniform.

George shrugged at her usual display of impatience and was pleased to see that it had no effect on the man greeting them.

"Welcome aboard, Mr. and Mrs. Porter. My name is Ken Boslow. I'm the ship's purser. I believe you're the first of your company to board. You are all quartered on B deck. The steward will show you to your cabin and your luggage will be deposited there shortly."

"Thank you, Mr. Boslow. I'm sure we're in for a pleasant trip." George nodded as he retrieved their papers from the purser.

"And just where does one get a drink, Mr. Boslow?" Harriet scowled.

With the broadest of smiles, the purser replied, "Complimentary champagne and fruit are provided in every cabin, Mrs. Porter, and embarkation refreshments will be served in the Lotus Ballroom as soon as we're underway." He checked his watch. "In exactly ninety minutes."

"Humph, I should hope so," Harriet replied.

As she and George turned to follow their steward, they were startled by a second greeting. "Welcome aboard. Awk, welcome aboard."

"What in the world is this?" Harriet shrieked. She stood facing a bright green parrot with a yellow head perched on the railing. Cocking its head to one side, it looked at Harriet and took a few steps closer. "Awk, welcome aboard," it said again.

"I'll be darned!" George exclaimed. "What a beautiful bird!"

"I can see it's a bird, George, but just what the heck is it doing on our ship?"

"That's Taco, ma'am," the steward explained. "He's kind of... part of... the crew."

*   *   *

Marge and Bill Collin, boarded shortly after the Porters, followed by Jean Dawson and her husband, Jim.

"Welcome aboard, Mr. and Mrs. Collin, Mr. And Mrs. Dawson." The purser handed their papers back to them. "The Porters arrived earlier and are being escorted to their cabin. You are all on B deck. Please enjoy our ship." The width of his smile remained fixed.

"That figures," Bill Collin said to the others. "Poor George probably had to get up and check out at dawn."

Jean Dawson grinned. "Harriet was griping all the way down here on the flight last night. I've never seen anyone who could find so much to complain about."

"Now, now," Bill's wife chided, "let's make this a pleasant voyage, personalities and politics aside." She straightened his collar.

"That won't be all that easy, Marge. Knowing Yvonne, she probably detests the whole idea."

"And you all thought this was a pleasure trip," Jean Dawson quipped.

"There's Barry and Helen Miller." Collin waved when he spotted them ascending the gangplank.

Simon Dumont and his wife, Dina, were a few steps behind the Millers.

"As soon as our beloved leaders make their customary late entrance," Jean Dawson commented, "the entire Silvers crew will be ready for a sail into perdition. What a cruise this is going to be," she quickly added.

A few seconds later they were also greeted by Taco, "Welcome aboard. Awk, welcome aboard." He rocked back and forth on the railing as he continued to welcome each passenger.

They chuckled as the steward led them below.

CHAPTER 7

The Lotus Ballroom

Most of the ship's passengers were now mingling in the Lotus Ballroom located to the rear of the promenade deck. A huge chandelier of hand blown, multi-colored glass globules dominated the room. All the furnishings, chairs, tables and bar areas were fabricated from thick oriental bamboo. Lotus flower-shaped lighting sconces hung evenly spaced on the walls that were papered in a pink and green striped pattern. Sand-colored carpeting complemented and completed the entire tropical effect.

Shortly after getting the ship safely underway, the captain joined his passengers. A broad-chested man of around fifty-five, he exuded six feet of authority and confidence as he addressed them. "Welcome, ladies and gentlemen," he spoke up amidst the clinking of glasses and mixed chatter. "I am Capt. John Markem and I toast your choice of the Coral Queen." He held up a champagne flute. "The Queen is the smallest of our fleet but she's by far the biggest when it comes to your total cruise enjoyment. It will be my pleasure and responsibility, and that of the crew, to see that each of you has a most pleasant and memorable voyage."

"I'll bet he's said that hundreds of times before," Harriet scoffed as she sampled her first drink of the day. The rest of the Silvers group simply ignored her.

"Here, here." The clinking of glasses followed the voice of one of the passengers assembled in the teak-paneled ballroom. Appearing to join the toast, the captain barely touched the bubbling liquid to his lips.

After a few minutes more of excited and joyful passenger chatter, Capt. Markem got their attention again by tapping his glass with a spoon. "I promise this will be my last announcement," he declared. "Because they will be seeing to your every need, I would like to introduce my officers and the senior members of my crew." He directed their attention to the starched looking gentleman of about forty sporting a huge British colonial moustache who was standing next to him. "This is First Mate Roger Wills. Roger is also the ship's security officer."

"Welcome aboard. I would like to point out, not that you should have any concerns, however, that we do advise you utilize the safe in your rooms for all valuables." The First Mate casually twisted one end of his mustache and raised his glass with the other.

"Well said, Roger." The captain then turned a palm to his left, "Our ship's doctor, Dr. Gwen Gordon."

"Welcome aboard." A petite woman in her fifties with short, salt and pepper hair, wearing a slightly loose-fitting uniform greeted them. "You all look quite healthy, so please stay that way." Her quip evoked a response of laughter and more clinking of glasses. "And if you haven't been greeted by our ship's mascot," the doctor was holding the parrot perched on her left forearm, "this is Taco." She lifted her arm slightly.

Right on cue, the bird said loudly, "Greetings and welcome aboard. Awk."

More laughter resounded as several passengers returned his greeting.

"As you can see," the captain chortled, "in addition to being one of the finest physicians on land or sea, the doctor has a great sense of humor and a love for all living creatures. I'm sure you'll find little Taco to be a friendly and amusing crew-member during your cruise. Except for the dining rooms, he has full run of the ship."

The captain continued his introductions. "And, of course, Dr. Gordon is capably assisted by our nurse, Jamie Brewer." He smiled in the direction of a youngish-looking woman in a fitted ship's uniform. She brushed her hand across her close-cropped brown hair as the captain continued. "Nurse Brewer also has the added responsibility of Ship and Shore Activities Director."

"Thank you, Captain. Welcome aboard, everyone," she greeted. "You'll find an activities schedule posted in your rooms with my shipboard phone number. Please feel free to participate as often or as little as you like."

Capt. Markem went on, "You've all met our purser, Ken Boslow." Boslow gave a friendly nod.

"And the one you'll most appreciate on the Coral Queen, our Head Chef, Andre Franc."

Attired in the pure white garb of a gourmet chef, thin, cherry-faced Chef Andre smiled. "Welcome. Lunch will be available at two buffet tables aboard ship. Their locations are posted in your rooms. Breakfast and brunch will also be served there. My staff will be happy to accommodate any special dietary requests. As for dinner, it will be formal and begins at seven in the Golden Palms Dining Room. Bon appétit!"

"Bon appétit!" echoed Taco.

"Now, ladies and gentlemen, enjoy your cruise and all the amenities we have to offer." The captain replaced his cap, gave a brief salute and left the ballroom. The senior crew-members then circulated among those passengers who remained to enjoy more champagne and hors d'oeuvres.

*   *   *

Following the captain's greeting ceremony, Mel and Yvonne Silvers welcomed their guests as they congregated together in one corner of the ballroom. "I just wish to say that Yvonne and I plan to become better acquainted with all of you on a more personal level on this little excursion. It will also serve as a reward for your diligent efforts that have made Silvers such a great success."

At sixty, even with his pure silver-white hair, a product of his own labs, and his casual tailor-made wardrobe of pin-striped blazer and white trousers, Mel still had the appearance of a well-dressed little boy, in spite of his title and position of authority in the company. They all nodded amiably at his comments, each hoping he or she would be selected to be the next Senior VP at Silvers.

As usual, it was Yvonne Silvers who broke the festive mood when she seized their full attention. "It won't, however, be all play," she quickly added. "I intend for us to spend time discussing the future growth of Silvers."

It was becoming harder and harder for Mel to deal with Yvonne's total disregard for the feelings of others. It was no secret within the industry that Yvonne's family money had started the business and that she, as Chairperson, was the demanding helms-woman of Silvers Cosmetics. It was also obvious to all who knew them that Mel's sole function as CEO was to stroke the staff and charm Silvers' elite cosmetics retailers. Having no real taste or fortitude for the ruthless, competitive, nature of the cosmetics business, he had been fulfilling that role willingly, but now her overbearing dominance was making his minor duties more difficult to perform.

"Well then, that being said," Mel concluded, "I suggest we enjoy the remainder of the day. See you all at dinner." He took Yvonne's elbow and escorted her to their stateroom.

*   *   *

"I figured there was more to this trip than the pre-launch sessions," Jean Dawson exclaimed. "As usual, Mel pours the honey and she serves the vinegar."

"Like I told you," Barry Miller interjected, "they'll be evaluating us to determine who is to replace Herb."

"And lucky old Herb is now head of a large health and beauty company. As upset as he was, he seemed almost relieved when he left," George Porter added.

"Still, it's going to be an interesting cruise. And may the best man win."

"Hey!" Jean Dawson complained.

"Okay, I mean best person. See you all at dinner." Bill Collin turned heel to leave. His wife, Marge, smiled and followed.

"And here's to a wonderful repast tonight," Simon Dumont toasted his fellow associates as they broke up. "Come on, Dina, let's explore this floating resort."

CHAPTER 8

Executive Suite 1B-The Silvers

"Yvonne, you could have let this promotion business sit for the first day or two."

"Are you sure this is the best accommodation on board, Mel? This room looks rather skimpy," she yelled from the adjoining bedroom. "In fact this whole ship, if you can call it that, seems a little on the skimpy side to me. Since you dragged me on this compassionate cruise of yours, you could have at least chosen a real ship."

"The Coral Queen is considered an elite cruise ship for corporations like ours. This is the executive suite on the sundeck level and the best accommodation on board. And you're doing it again, Yvonne, avoiding my opinion."

Wrapped in a gray Gucci robe, she joined him in the small sitting room that separated their bedrooms.

"Would you care for some champagne?" He lifted the complimentary bottle from the ice bucket.

Ignoring his offer, Yvonne unwrapped the complimentary fruit basket and popped a large lush grape into her mouth. She spoke as she chewed. "That's because your opinions always miss the point. Why delay the inevitable? We both know who I think should replace that ingrate, Herb Marshall. I'm sure he'll never make it at that dumb soap company he went with."

Mel kicked off his Bally loafers and put his feet up on a blue suede chair. "It's not a soap company. Global is the second largest health and beauty company in the country. We lost a good man with Herb, and I think you're totally out of line by not wanting to pay him his bonus."

"Why give a deserting rat a reward? You're too eager to give him $150,000 of our money." She continued to poke through the fruit basket.

"You know he'll sue us for it."

"Let him. He'll chew some of it up in legal fees."

"I'll never understand how you can treat people the way you do. And you know I'm against your choice for his replacement. You realize that after this, Yvonne, keeping a high morale among the people who helped make this company successful is going to be extremely difficult."

"That empathy of yours is the only reason I allowed you to arrange this ridiculous cruise."

"I just think it will be easier for them to digest your news in this environment rather than in our conference room. They deserve at least that much consideration."

She grabbed a small cluster of grapes and headed toward the bathroom, "Just remember, it's Silvers in name only and my controlling interest means my instincts are always right. That's more than I can say about some people."

He grabbed a banana and waved it at her like a pistol. "Someday, Yvonne Rosen, you're going to find out just how important you really aren't."

"Eat your banana, you dumb ape, I'm taking a shower. And be sure my trinkets are locked in that safe," she bellowed slamming the bathroom door behind her.

CHAPTER 9

Suite 4B- The Porters

"Two windows, is that all the Vice President of Operations rates?" Harriet Porter hadn't been in their suite five minutes when she started evaluating the mistreatment she had anticipated from her first step onto the gangplank. In spite of her complaining, the room was quite comfortable and well appointed, even if a bit tight for space.

"Sometimes, Harriet, I wonder just what will please you," George replied. "When Bill Collin booked this trip, he showed me an accommodation layout. B deck is the premium level on the ship and this is one of the finest rooms available."

She plopped down on the white divan and pawed through their fruit basket. "I'll bet her almighty, Queen Yvonne, has better."

"Don't start, Harriet. These next few days are just as important to you as they are to me."

"Well I just can't stand her flaunting ways. I mean, who wears a huge emerald necklace at nine in the morning?" Ignoring the fruit, she drained the remaining champagne from the flute she had carried back from the welcoming reception.

"You know she loves jewelry. Besides, who cares if Mel and Yvonne have a better room? After all, they do own the company, which does allow for some extra privileges."

Seated on the edge of his bed, he removed his wing tips and wiggled his toes.

"You mean she-e-e owns the company, including Mel and all the rest of you poor fools."

George stared at his wife and wondered if the entire week was going to be one complaint after another. But then, he knew his wife, of course, and was certain that, after a few martinis, he would again have to be a buffer between her and Yvonne. "Let's try to make the best of this voyage, Harriet, in spite of Yvonne."

"Not with that woman so close by. Honestly, George, if you don't get the promotion, I'll let her have it for sure."

"Don't worry, Harriet. The best thing that could have happened, as far as I'm concerned, was for Herb to resign or be fired. If it hadn't been for Mel knowing better, Herb would have taken all the credit for the success of my Honey Pot Crème and I'm sure that Mel feels I'm the most likely candidate for his replacement." He removed his sport shirt, grabbed their bottle of champagne from the ice bucket and patted his bed, inviting her to join him. "Let's relax a little before dinner."

She held her forehead, "Sorry, George, too much champagne already." She proceeded to hang her clothes.

With no hope of an affectionate response on her part, he replaced the bottle in the ice bucket. Tempted to light up his pipe, but knowing that would only make matters worse, he rolled over and took a nap.

CHAPTER 10

Suite 5B- The Collins

"I'm glad to see our luggage is here." Marge Collin went immediately to unpacking their bags. "Don't toss your jacket on the bed like that, Bill." She picked it up and hung it in one of the two closets in the room.

"Do you have to fuss the minute we get here, Marge? Try to relax and enjoy this short vacation," Bill said, knowing his urging was a waste of effort.

"You know I can't tolerate disorder." She continued organizing their clothes. "Besides, if I don't look after you, who will?"

"I know, Marge." He wrapped his arms around her full waist. At six feet, he stood two inches above her. They had met in college when he was a sophomore and she was a junior and a year older. Although he was only fifty, her motherly ways often made him feel much younger. "What do you say we put on our swim suits, head for the ship's spa, have a drink and slip into the hot tub?"

He was still hugging her as she lined up socks and under-things in the dressers.

"Nobody's going to run an inspection to see if everything's neat and in order, Marge. Can't you just relax a little bit this once?"

"This will only take another minute, but no hot tub for me. The moist heat will ruin my new hairdo."

"Whatever," he released her. "Hand me my trunks and let's get out of here before you rearrange the furniture."

"You just don't appreciate me, do you, Bill?"

He watched her. Although she was a bit on the heavy side, she was still appealing. Such thoughts were brief, however, as she painstakingly hung her dress and slipped into a terry beach jumper.

"You should bear in mind, Mr. VP of Sales, that my looking after you and your neat appearance might help get you the promotion to Senior VP."

"I guess I have a pretty good shot at it. It's hard to tell what those two are thinking."

"You'd better have more than a shot at it for all the good you've done for Silvers. I'll be one unhappy camper if you don't, and they'll know it."

"You and me both. But for now, let's enjoy ourselves." He laid his slacks neatly on the bed to avoid any further fussing on her part and drew on his trunks. "You know, Marge, I'll bet I'm the only one on board with creases in his swimming trunks."

CHAPTER 11

Suite 6B- The Millers

"I really hated to leave the kids behind, Barry. I know your folks love having them, but they do spoil them rotten." Helen Miller was staring out one of the windows at the open sea.

"How they can spoil a thirteen and sixteen-year-old who have it all is not my concern right now, dear, and if anything, it's my parents who will be spoiled. Now that she can drive, Jenny will take them back and forth to the mall, and Susie will insist they eat out every night. I just hope my Dad's stomach is ready for lots of pizza."

"Stop exaggerating." She smiled as she turned from the expansive view of the sea. "Okay, I know how important these next few days are to you and I know the kids will be fine. I'll just call later and give them our ship-to-shore number." She checked the bedside phone for a dial tone.

"This is going to be a tough trip for me, Helen. It's hard enough to deal with Yvonne, the egomaniac, and the rest of our so-called executives, during the course of daily business, but to have to socialize and kowtow... it won't be easy."

"How about me? You know I can't stand Yvonne with all her jewels and furs. And Jean Dawson, how she got to be VP of Merchandising isn't too hard to figure out," she said facetiously.

"Merchandising, that's a crock," he retorted as he undressed to take a shower. "My group does all the marketing planning and she gets it all handed to her on a platter. It's a meaningless position and one I'll eliminate as Senior VP," he declared as he stepped into the tiny stall.

Helen could never get used to seeing the scar on his back, the souvenir of a Vietnamese bullet. She was very proud of Barry and shuddered at what might have happened. He had been a Marine Captain when they married and, at sixty-two, he still carried himself like one. Erect and proud with a brown crew cut, he was still the man she had loved back then, and she maintained her youthful appearance for that very reason. Her jet black hair and hazel eyes were the two things he always claimed had won his heart, but she was also aware that a decent figure was part of the attraction, and she intended to keep it that way even after having given birth twice. She was also aware of how important it was for the wife of a successful cosmetics executive to look the part, perfectly coiffed, perfectly dressed, and most important, perfectly made up.

CHAPTER 12

Suite 7B- The Dawsons

"You know, Jean, it's really great that your company is taking us on this cruise. It'll give you a chance to unwind a little." Jim Dawson held open the door to their room.

"Just shut the darn door, Jim."

Once inside, he spotted the large, bright, cello-wrapped fruit basket and champagne. "Isn't this thoughtful!"

"Oh please! You have no idea what's in store for me during the next few days, and a bunch of fruit isn't going to compensate for it."

He hated when she was like this and secretly blamed it on her career choice. He fully imagined how difficult it must be for a woman in such a competitive industry, especially with all the travel involved. How she could even face the hassle of commuting into the city every day was beyond him.

It wasn't like that for him though. Running the bookstore was a dull life according to Jean, but he had always loved books. The personal contact and easy-going environment in their small hometown of Elmwood, New Jersey, suited him just fine. Jean often commented on the contrast between them. She had always been the aggressive, adventurous one. Even when they had been in high school and then junior college, she had thrived on trying exciting new things and was totally involved in as many extracurricular activities as she could fit into her schedule.

And popular, she had certainly been that as well. Her Scandinavian features, light brown hair and athletic figure, captured as much attention as any young woman could possibly desire.

To this day, Jim could hardly believe she had been attracted to him. He often wondered if his being quiet and unassuming was one of the reasons she had chosen him. He had never really been a lady's man, but his good looks and tall stature had often caused women to cast flirtatious eyes in his direction. None of them had seriously attracted his attention. He had loved Jean from the moment he first saw her and he still felt the same way. There was nothing he wouldn't do for her happiness, even to foregoing the family he had always hoped for.

Vibrating with nervous energy, Jean quickly unpacked and, after hanging her things in her closet, settled in a leather side-chair and lit a cigarette, which always annoyed him.

"You know, Jean, now that we're in our forties, shouldn't you consider that smoking is a high risk pleasure, not only for you, but for nonsmokers around you as well?"

She swung her long legs over the arm of the chair, took a long drag and crushed out the butt. "It helps relax me, Jim, just like your wine in the evening."

"Wine is good for the heart and, besides, the Surgeon General…"

She was flipping through a shipboard booklet ignoring him. Sunshine streaming through the windows danced across the textured carpet as she tossed the booklet aside. "What do you say we put on some deck clothes and take a little tour?"

"Sounds good, and by then, it'll be lunchtime."

"Wear that new blue-checked shirt I bought you at Brooks Brothers," she advised.

CHAPTER 13

Suite 8B- The Dumonts

"I don't understand you, Simon, your creative efforts in both design and advertising have made millions for Mel and Her Highness, Yvonne. And now you're sipping that champagne and telling me you don't expect to have a chance at the Senior VP slot."

Dina Dumont was slightly taller than her husband, but she towered over him now as he sat and listened to her.

Adjusting the collar of his cashmere turtleneck, he replied, "Why in heaven's name would I want that kind of job anyway? It mostly entails financial and leadership skills that I don't have and would hate to have."

She started pacing their room, a sure sign that she wasn't finished with the subject. They had been married twelve years and by now he was sure he knew her every mood, her every gesture. In spite of her constant nagging that he better himself, he still loved and needed her and did his best to please her. Dina was a definite asset to him in his world of fashion. Her striking good looks, well-coifed auburn hair, and tight body always drew compliments at social and business functions.

"You told me once there wasn't anything you couldn't do if you put your mind to it." She placed her hands on her trim hips.

"Oh, now look at that." He held up his finger. He'd gotten a paper cut from the cello as he tried to remove a pear from their fruit basket. Twisting a paper napkin around it, he said, "I meant when it comes to a form of art, or a clever way of portraying glamorous, fashionable women, or even sculpting a piece of clay into the shape of a fragrance bottle. I didn't mean being in charge of these other VPs who would be depending on my decisions for success."

"Nonsense, Simon, you're responsible for art directors, fashion photographers and copywriters. I don't see any big difference."

"Please, Dina, keep your ambitious desires to boost me into a world of misery to yourself. End of discussion. Got it?" His French temper was near boiling.

"We'll see about that. How quickly you've forgotten who encouraged you to leave Cosmo Cosmetics to take the VP slot you now enjoy at Silvers." She wasn't about to let it go.

The napkin around his finger was soaked. "This darn thing is still bleeding. I'm going to the infirmary for a bandage." He headed for the door.

"What better image could there be for Silvers than to have a talented Frenchman as Senior VP? Think about it. It's the prestige, Simon, the prestige," she yelled after him.

CHAPTER 14

The Infirmary

"Just a little antiseptic and a small adhesive bandage should do nicely, Mr. Dumont."

Simon felt silly perched on the end of the examining table. "I feel foolish about coming down here, but neither my wife nor I bothered to pack any Band-aids."

"Nonsense, sir. That's why we're here."

Simon was always uncomfortable in examining rooms, not so much from a medical necessity standpoint, but they all had that same sterile feel which disturbed his creative sensitivity. He always likened such rooms of angular stainless steel fixtures to the Art Deco period. He much preferred the Art Nouveau style of soft and sweeping curves.

"Thanks, Nurse. By the way, that's one smart bird perched out there in the outer office. He said, 'You're next,' when I walked in."

"Yeah, Taco's a smart one all right. Sometimes he's too smart for his own good."

"I take it you don't care for parrots."

"Oh sure I do. It's just that he's a bit too nosy some-times."

"Too nosy, Taco's too nosy. Awk."

"He certainly doesn't seem to have a hearing problem," Simon laughed.

"See what I mean?" Nurse Brewer couldn't help smiling.

"What's this, our first casualty and only four hours out to sea, Jamie?" Dr. Gordon entered the infirmary.

"Mr. Dumont had a tussle with our fruit basket's cello wrap, Doctor."

"It's just a paper cut, but it kept bleeding and I didn't have a Band-aid..." He slid off the examining table.

"You did the right thing, Mr. Dumont. The last passenger who was attacked by our fruit basket had to be buried at sea."

Simon smiled. He always considered that a good sense of humor was a sign of professional confidence, and these two impressed him as being very confident. "Thanks for the extra bandages, Nurse." He held up his finger. "She did a good job, Doctor."

"We're fortunate to have Jamie, Mr. Dumont. After ten years as a Navy nurse, you would think she'd have had enough of seafaring care."

"It's the salt air, actually," Jamie quipped as she stowed away the first aid kit. "Besides, this sure beats carrier duty."

"We'll check you out at dinner," Dr. Gordon told him. "I believe your group is the first to join us at the Captain's Table this evening."

"Check you at dinner, awk."

As he passed the bird on his way out, Simon stopped and said, "I don't think so. I understand you're not allowed in the dining room."

"Not allowed. Taco not allowed. Awk."

"It happens to everyone, Mr. Dumont," Dr. Gordon explained, "and it's contagious. You just can't help having a conversation with Taco."

Simon shook his head, amused that he had actually been involved in a conversation with a parrot. He chuckled and headed out to find Dina.

CHAPTER 15

The Sun Deck

Overhead the skies were deep blue and cloudless. A caressing warmth washed across the Sun Deck. Located at the forward end of the ship, the area was a sunbather's dream. Comfortable padded white lounges divided by bamboo side tables were spaced around a small canopied bar where the waiter was busy mixing and serving drinks to the few passengers relaxing there.

"That was quite a spread they put out." Barry was discreetly utilizing a toothpick as he commented on the lunch they had just enjoyed.

"Spread is the right word. That's what we'll all be doing if they keep feeding us like that." Helen was applying sun lotion.

"It is all so tempting, but the key is willpower," Marge chimed in as she neatly folded her towel.

"Have no fear," Bill replied. "After the meeting Mel and Yvonne plan for tomorrow, most of us will probably lose our appetites."

"Hell-o. Awk. Hell-o." Taco waddled toward their lounges.

"Hi there," Bill responded when the bird stopped right beside him. "You really do get around, don't you?"

"Get around. I get around. Awk."

"Bill, for heaven sakes, put your sandals under your lounge before that fool bird messes them up," Marge warned and then quickly proceeded to gather them up herself before he could.

"He's just being friendly, Marge." Bill watched as she tucked his sandals under her lounge.

"He does seem to be." Helen reached down to pet the bird.

"Be careful, Helen," Marge cautioned.

"Look at that, he likes being petted." Well aware of Marge's compulsive nature, she stroked the bird again.

"Likes being petted. Awk. Taco likes being petted."

They watched as he flapped his wings and flew up to the back of Helen's lounge. Perched there he cocked his head like a feathered eavesdropper.

"You're quite a little character, aren't you, fella?" Barry stood and stroked Taco's bright yellow head.

"Quite a character," Taco mimicked. Then he flew back down onto the deck and waddled away repeating, "Quite a character. Quite a character."

"Did you hear that, Jean?" Jim Dawson asked as they passed the bird. He turned to watch as Taco greeted other passengers.

"Hi, guys," she said as they joined the Collins and the Millers. "How exciting, a talking parrot."

"Pull up a lounge and relax while we're still able," Bill invited.

"Thanks, maybe later. Jim's pretty hungry. We haven't had lunch yet."

"Be prepared, Jim. They weren't kidding when they said the cruise food was fabulous."

"Abundant, is more the case." Barry tapped his gut.

"And where are Her Highness and Mel?" Jean asked.

"Knowing her, they probably ordered room service so she wouldn't have to eat with the hired help. As we were leaving the breakfast room, we did see George and Harriet, along with Simon and Dina, filling their plates. They're joining us by the pool later." Marge reached to adjust her husband's towel.

Helen shook her head in amusement over Marge's doting attention to Bill's every need.

CHAPTER 16

The Lido Pool

Except for Mel and Yvonne, the entire Silvers group was seated by the pool. The white lounges there were similar to the ones on the sun deck except for the small adjustable umbrellas attached to the back of each chair for shade against the bright sunshine. Simon was shooting his associates from various angles with his Nikon.

"Simon, how many shots do you intend to take?" Dina protested as she dangled her feet in the hot tub that adjoined the oval pool.

"Hey Simon, how about some real glamour stuff?" Barry called out as he made a show of muscle.

"I figure I might as well have a record of all you happy people before tomorrow's big meeting," Simon said capturing Barry's pose.

"I for one don't really care which one of us they choose," Jean Dawson exclaimed. "After all we've been through together building this company, whoever it is will be a pleasure to work for."

Bill Collin smiled faintly. He knew she wasn't all that sincere. He, as well as the others, was aware that she was Mel's favorite.

"I have to say that I'm not all that happy about any part of this cruise," Harriet Porter complained. "First of all, we were given hardly any notice. I mean, how can one prepare for a cruise in just a few days? I had almost no time to acquire proper attire. It was just very inconsiderate of them to expect us to be ready on such short notice. Besides, who cruises this time of year?"

"Not many, evidently," Helen Miller finally got a word in. "Have you noticed there aren't that many passengers on board?"

"Ah-h, there's a good reason for that; it's the off-season," Bill Collin said, "and most cruise companies offer great discounts. Need I say more? Because bookings are off, I managed to get suites which were discounted even more."

Harriet elbowed her husband, "I told you it was something like that, George, didn't I?" She looked around. "Has anyone seen a waiter?" she asked.

He shrugged his shoulders. "Even so, you must admit that it's quite pleasant now that we're here." He stroked Harriet's arm as if that would calm her down.

"You're too easily satisfied," she retorted. "If I didn't…"

"Hey! Look who just arrived in time for a photo," Dina announced to break the tension as Taco waddled over and perched atop the arm of George's lounge.

Simon got a great shot of George and Taco staring at each other. They looked as though they were communicating silently.

"He's a regular little ham. I believe he likes posing for pictures," Barry said.

"Little ham," Taco repeated as he preened his feathers and posed again.

That broke them all up, except for Marge Collin. "I wonder who cleans up after him?" She looked around as if expecting to see a messy deck.

"Come on, Marge, it's just a parrot. I'm sure he's ship-broken."

They all laughed at Jean's response.

CHAPTER 17

The Royal Palm Dining Room

The Royal Palm Dining Room was barely half occupied. Situated in the forward section of the main deck, it was encircled by windows on three sides that, because of the darkness of night, mirrored the activity inside. Light ecru table linens contrasted delicately with the overall décor. Red upholstered chairs blended well with the coral carpeting, and the flocked wallpaper with a subtle palm tree motif in shades of pale greens gave decorating credence to the room's name. Overhead in the center of the room a ten-foot diameter frosted glass dome surrounded by smaller satellite domes glowed like moonlight upon the diners below, while table lamps in the form of palm fronds provided the proper amount of lighting. Soft background music absorbed most of the noise created by the chatter of the diners and waiters working their way to and from the kitchen.

On this the first night out, the Silvers Cosmetics group was seated at the Captain's Table. It was seven-thirty and, except for two empty seats, they were all there with the ship's senior crew interspersed among them.

Being the statesman that he must be at all times, Capt. Markem proposed a toast while they waited for the arrival of Yvonne and Mel Silvers. Raising his champagne flute, he said, "Here's to a pleasant evening and a truly enjoyable cruise."

George Porter was first to respond, "Thank you, Captain." He raised his flute in return.

Jean Dawson seconded, "Yes, thank you, Captain."

Harriet's impatience was evident when she burst into the toasts. "While we're being kept waiting by the Silvers, Captain, I must ask a question."

"Of course, Mrs. Porter." Remembering your guests' names is another requirement of a good captain. "What is it?" Capt. Markem could see all the others cringe at what unexpected comment might come out of her oversized lips.

"Just how many passengers does this ship accommodate?"

"The Queen is considered a prestige ship and most of our bookings are exclusive corporate or seminar cruises. She only carries one hundred and fifty passengers with a crew of seventy-five for the ultimate in passenger service," he answered for the benefit of them all.

"And how many passengers are on this cruise?" she continued.

The captain glanced at Ken Boslow.

"We'll be boarding seven more when we dock in San Juan day after tomorrow. They're associated with the insurance group already on board," Boslow informed him.

"Then that will be a total of eighty-six," the captain replied.

"That's not very many. You're only a little over half-full. I don't see how you can run a profitable business that way," Harriet insisted. "I would think it would be more economical to only sail at full capacity."

"Unfortunately, it doesn't work that way, Mrs. Porter. Even during the off-season, like the airlines and rail systems, we must maintain a schedule to accommodate those who have booked with us."

"Humph." She studied her nearly empty martini glass.

"Nonetheless, Mrs. Porter," First Mate Roger Wills added, "we still have our full complement of crew which will only enhance the service and enjoyment you will receive since there are fewer passengers."

The captain nodded at Wills' logic, then declared happily, "Ah, here are Mr. and Mrs. Silvers now."

They all looked up to watch Yvonne and Mel make their entrance. As usual, Yvonne was impeccably dressed. Strung around her surgically smooth throat was a necklace of clustered diamonds beautifully set off by her deep purple evening dress.

"Sorry we're late, everyone," Mel apologized as he pulled out Yvonne's chair.

But the griping had just begun. Yvonne didn't sit down. She remained standing. "I must tell you, Captain, our tardiness is totally due to my exhaustion after that foolish drill we were put through earlier. As a result, I overslept my nap."

Accustomed to demanding passengers, the captain replied politely, "It is a rather cumbersome routine, I know, Mrs. Silvers, but…"

"Cumbersome is hardly the word for those horrible, uncomfortable orange jackets we were instructed to put on," she interrupted as she finally took her seat.

"They are that," he continued without losing it, "but maritime regulations require a safety drill as soon as we're at sea. I am sorry it tired you."

"Well, I do hope that's the last of it. I'm certainly not going through that every time we leave port," she declared, her tone of voice clearly reflecting her intention to avoid further discomfort of any kind.

"Absolutely not." He signaled the waiters to start taking dinner orders.

The subject was ended on a lighter note when Simon humorously suggested a paisley print life jacket rather than plain orange.

"Mr. Dumont is a designer, Captain," Dr. Gordon explained. "He's also our first shipboard casualty."

"Oh?" The captain studied Simon.

"Cello wrap cut from a difficult fruit basket." Simon held up his bandaged finger.

During dinner, conversation was quiet and cordial between those seated next to one another. It wasn't until coffee was served that everyone's attention was ultimately drawn to Dina's question to Dr. Gordon.

"I'm curious, Doctor," she began, "about the parrot, Taco. How did he come to be living on board this ship?"

"Yeah, how 'bout that bird, Doctor?" Harriet slurred. She was on her third martini with no interest whatsoever in the coffee being offered.

Turning to face the captain, she addressed him directly, "I find it very irregular that you have a bird aboard ship, Captain." She had the snobbish habit, unless it was to her benefit, of only addressing people of the highest authority as she considered herself to be.

"I think you'll all find Dr. Gordon's explanation of how Taco became a member of our crew rather interesting as well as humane," he smiled.

"Who really cares about the details of how he got here?" Yvonne said to Mel. "I'm ready for a stroll before retiring. Are you coming?"

"I want to hear," he whispered back. "If you want to stroll now, go ahead. I'll join you on deck shortly."

"Then stay," she said testily. "Thank you for dinner, Captain." Ignoring everyone else, she rose and left without waiting to hear his response.

"Taco's really a dear little fellow," the doctor began. "About two years ago, we were on a corporate cruise in the gulf..."

The captain interrupted to explain, "The Queen is available primarily for exclusive group cruises. I believe the one Dr. Gordon is referring to was a food brokers meeting and a computer company's tech seminar."

"We were anchored off the shore of the Yucatan Peninsula and there was a heavy storm during the night," she continued. "The next morning one of the crew found poor Taco. He had obviously been blown onto our deck and he was soaking wet. He looked as if he had been battered badly by the strong winds. Of course, he was brought to me in the infirmary. The poor thing was frightened half to death, and when I examined him, I discovered he had a broken wing."

"For a people doctor," Jamie interjected, "she did a great job patching him up."

"Don't worry, folks, I'm still a better people doctor than a bird doctor," she promised. "At any rate, it took about two weeks for him to mend enough to remove the splint I put on him. It was then I could see that there was some permanent wing damage that allowed him to fly very short distances only. In fact, his perch in my quarters is about as high as he can manage. Such a limitation for a bird his size is a real handicap. He makes up for it, however, in intelligence and sociability. So there you have it, we adopted him, and he's been a happy member of the crew ever since."

"I guess if you're going to have a mascot on board, a parrot seems most appropriate," Simon commented. "After all, it was common practice to have parrots on pirate ships and other old sailing vessels."

"There's some truth to that," the captain replied. "But from what I've read, the sailors captured them and brought them on board to sell in less exotic ports. In the case of the Yellow-Headed Amazons like Taco, their ability to retain a rather extensive vocabulary and mimic human speech brought higher prices. And I must say, whoever trained him before he came on board taught him to the full extent of his word-stock." Having finished dinner, the captain stood. "I would like to thank you for joining me this evening. Now, if you will excuse me, I must be heading for the bridge."

"Thank you and good night, Captain," Mel said. "Speaking for all of us, we appreciate your hospitality."

"All but Her Highness," Harriet whispered to George.

"Looks like this party is breaking up. Anyone for a drink in the Lounge?" Barry suggested.

Jean and Jim accepted. Everyone else dispersed for the evening.

CHAPTER 18

The Ship's Card Room

"That was some breakfast," Bill Collin declared as he studied the card room he had reserved. The room had been rearranged for their small group meeting about which they were all so apprehensive. Several tables had been placed together covered by a large piece of dark green felt. Chairs were spaced around the table that held pads, pens and pencils, a water pitcher, glasses, carafes of coffee and tea, and china cups. Collin was satisfied with the set-up. The lighting was good and the pleasant earth tones of the carpeting and upholstery, along with the whimsical tropical motif wallpaper, gave the room a warm ambience.

"What's Marge up to while we're all stuck here for a cruel morning at sea?" Barry asked as they all entered the card room.

"Getting her nails done along with Dina, I believe," Bill replied as he adjusted the chairs.

"At least our spouses will enjoy the next few hours," Jean grouched.

"Don't tell me Jim's getting his nails done, too," Simon teased as he took a shot out the broad window located at the forward end of the room.

"Very funny, Simon." Jean poured herself a cup of coffee.

"I guess this is it." George was the last to arrive, except for Yvonne and Mel.

While they moved about the room waiting, an unexpected visitor came through the open door and perched on the back of the chair at the head of the table. "Awk, good morning, everyone."

"Look at that," Simon declared. "Maybe he's going to be our new Senior VP."

"Nothing will surprise me this morning." George walked toward where Taco was perched. "I don't think you'll be too welcome here by our faultless leader, old boy." He shifted the pipe in his mouth and extended his arm. The bird flapped onto it.

"I'll be darned," Jean blurted, "we have an animal trainer in our midst."

"Not really," he replied. "However, I did have a summer job in a pet shop when I was seventeen and they had a cockatoo that liked to perch on my shoulder whenever I was in the shop. Besides, I think Taco likes the smell of my tobacco." Walking to the door, he gently set the parrot down. "Off you go, Taco."

As the bird waddled, away he sang out, "Off you go, Taco. Off you go."

A few minutes later Mel joined them taking the seat next to Jean. "Yvonne's running a bit late. As you all know, she likes to sleep in."

"That's because of her nightly cognac," Barry whispered to Simon.

"While we wait, I'd like to tell you all once again how pleased we are with this year's sales results."

There were a few nods of acceptance as Bill volunteered, "You did more than your share to help pull it off, Mel."

"It's a team effort, but more importantly, you'll find how pleased we are when bonuses are distributed... ah, here's Yvonne now," he broke off.

"Bonuses? You're discussing bonuses?" she exclaimed as she approached the empty chair at the end of the table.

"They're not due until next month and that's certainly not the subject of this meeting."

"Here, Yvonne, allow me." Bill slid her chair out.

"Kissing up doesn't suit you, Mr. Collin." She plopped into the chair.

He wasn't embarrassed by her rude show of disrespect. They had learned to expect it. She treated them all the same way. He took his seat, however, wishing he had pulled the chair out from under her. The mere image in his mind of her bouncing off the floor made him smile.

"Pour some coffee for me, Mel," she demanded. Shading her eyes, she further ordered, "And someone pull the blinds on that fool window, the glare's annoying."

Simon, who was the closest, joked as he redirected the rays toward the ceiling, "There goes your morning radiance, Yvonne."

"Idiot," she mumbled as she stirred her coffee.

As usual, she took her time deliberately rearranging the pad, pens and pencils in front of her. While they waited for her to continue, the moments crawled like rush hour traffic on the Long Island Expressway.

After a few swallows of her coffee, she cleared her throat and said, "I know you're all wondering who's replacing that ingrate Herb. Well, you should know that, after taking into account all of our internal options, there is another candidate we are considering."

Mel's eyes were cast downward.

The shuffling of a few chairs broke the stunned silence that her announcement created.

"I don't understand!" Jean exclaimed.

"There's nothing to understand, Ms. Dawson. It's as simple as you can be at times, and don't you dare question my decision…"

"Perhaps I should explain," Mel interrupted quietly as he momentarily placed a supportive hand on Jean's trembling shoulder.

"Be my guest." Yvonne waved her hand indifferently in his direction, then drank more coffee.

"It's never an easy task when you're trying to choose from a balanced slate of candidates such as yourselves, especially when there are other factors that we must bear in mind…"

Yvonne interrupted, "I knew you'd try to soft-soap the issue, Mel, so let me get you off the proverbial meat hook." Then, with a determined look on her face, she added, "The decision will be all mine, and you all should know that Mel is not in accord with it."

"At least tell us who that person is," Barry finally spoke up.

"We do have a right to know, Yvonne," Bill insisted.

"The only right you people have is the right to do as you're told."

"Yvonne!" Mel scolded.

"All right, all right," she snapped. "We haven't made the offer yet and, until it's been accepted, you're not to discuss this with anyone outside of this room, so let's not have a lot of complaints and pouting. Is that clear?"

"Pouting creates crows-feet and we wouldn't want that, now would we?" Simon quipped.

No one found his remark the least bit humorous, especially Yvonne.

"Don't you dare mock me, you little Frenchman. Just stick to your colored crayons," she cut into him.

He fiddled with his camera in silence.

"So-o-o, tell us," George demanded.

"He's Stuart Rosen, my late brother's son. It'll all be resolved by the time we return to New York. In the meanwhile, I suggest you try to enjoy this little sojourn Mel insisted on."

Bill could read the hopelessness in Mel's eyes at the mention of Yvonne's nephew.

"Now I believe Mel has some marketing issues to discuss, which don't require my presence." She rose and left them abruptly with no concern over the shockwave she had created.

Through the doorway she had just exited, they heard her yell, "Get out of my way, you stupid bird!"

* * *

"Mel, I can't believe what just transpired here," Jean said. "How can you allow her to do this to us?"

"Easy, Jean, you must know by now the tough position she always puts Mel in," George answered before Mel could respond.

"It could be the good-for-nothing won't work out," Mel interjected a faint hope on his part.

"Good-for-nothing? Oh boy!" Barry exclaimed. "Just what do you mean, Mel?"

"Sounds like he's not on Mel's short list," Simon offered.

"Is that right, Mel?" Jean asked looking directly at him.

"I had one of you in mind, of course, but that's irrelevant now." Unlike Yvonne, he knew Silvers couldn't afford to lose any one of them and he felt he owed them some sort of an explanation. "I can tell you this, Stuart's father was Yvonne's deceased brother Myron's only son and, for personal reasons I can't get into, she feels some obligation toward him."

"That's not much of a reason to put him in such an important position," Bill contested.

"It's all I can say." Then Mel hesitated before adding, "They'll be discussing it over the next few days."

"You mean he's here on this ship?" Barry questioned.

"That's right," Mel admitted. "He has a suite on C deck. Yvonne thought it best to keep him under wraps, so to speak, until she broke the news to all of you."

"And when do we get to meet this nephew?" Simon inquired.

"When Yvonne decides," Mel told him.

"Is there any hope she'll reconsider?" Jean asked.

"When her mind's made up... well, you know Yvonne. Now is there anything else?" Mel asked somberly.

"Just one thing," Simon got their attention. "Here's the new container for our honey-based lip moisturizing cream." He removed a jar from a small sample case and set it before them. "If you recall, back in New York, I gave each of you a choice of two design samples filled with product. After each of you considered them for a few days, this is the jar design that was preferred. I'm quite pleased with your selection for, as you can see, the beehive texture of the opalescent glass truly enhances the pale honey color of the cream inside."

"Very nice, Simon; in fact, it's beautiful," Mel declared as he examined it closely. "And this is the new formula?" he asked.

"I believe so," George replied. "I understand Simon got it from our lab to be certain of the color consistency."

"Very well. I'll pass it by Yvonne just to be sure she concurs with all of us."

"Okay, that's it then." George was the first to get up and leave followed by Mel.

"I suppose so." Jean rose next.

The shuffling of other chairs followed and two minutes later the room was empty.

CHAPTER 19

Executive Suite 1B- The Silvers

When Mel returned to their suite, he found Yvonne's bedroom door closed. He tapped gently. "Yvonne, are you in there?"

"Who else would be? What is it?"

"Here's the new lip moisturizer design we've all agreed upon," he said as he entered.

"Just leave it on the table. I'm getting a headache."

"It doesn't surprise me you're not feeling well, Yvonne, after that terrible performance." He put the jar down and stood by her bed.

"This is not the time to aggravate me, Mel." She rolled onto her side.

He was determined to speak his mind. "It's one thing to tell them they may not be chosen for the job, and that you are planning to give it to your spoiled nephew, but you were blatantly crude about it."

She sat up. "I noticed how pained you looked when I put your pet, Ms. Merchandising, in her place."

"That's unfair, Yvonne. It's true I like Jean, but it's because she does a terrific job. Our in-store merchandising presence is the envy of the industry, thanks to her. It's a tough business and, as a woman, you should appreciate that."

"Spare me the analogy. She asked a dumb question and deserved my response."

"All right, let me try again. You know deep down Stuart's not right for this job, yet you're determined he have it, and you know that I know why."

"He's got a business degree from NYU." Her anger was escalating.

"For heaven sakes, Yvonne, he just barely graduated. He's lazy and spoiled. And what does he know about the cosmetics business?"

She got up and left him standing there while she went into the bathroom.

Whenever he was right, she left the room, made an unnecessary phone call, or complained of a headache, anything to avoid the issue.

"He's been working for Abe in his ready-to-wear coat company." She spoke through the bathroom door. "Besides, fashion is fashion, Mel," she added when she came out.

"Abe's his mother's brother and you know how that works. He's a spoiled twenty-nine year old. Supervising incoming material inspection, when he's there, is not exactly being a fashion expert." He sat on her bed to prevent her from lying back down. Having gotten this far, he wanted to get it all out.

"And what were you, Mel, before we started Silvers? A cosmetics buyer at Macy's." She stabbed back as she removed an emery board from her beauty bag and proceeded to file her nails, another maneuver to avoid looking at him during such disputes.

"That's not the point, and you know it. And if you remember, I was the head buyer and I applied myself."

"And now you're the head of the third largest cosmetics company in the country, thanks to me."

"You mean thanks to how you manipulated your parents' money. I know why you have this sudden urge to take Myron's boy under your wing. It's not guilt as much as fear that he'll pursue what Myron contended he was due right up until the poor man died."

"He wasn't entitled to any part of Silvers," she protested. "You know that they left me in charge of their estate. I returned his half of our inheritance years ago, in case you forgot."

"How can you be so callous, especially since he was legally helpless? He was entitled to more than that after you used his half to build a beauty empire. My God, Yvonne, you owed him millions, and now you think you can make it right by giving this position to his incompetent son? He'll louse things up for sure."

"No, he won't. I won't let that happen." She ousted him from where he was seated on her bed. "Now get out and let me rest."

"You're impossible, and somehow I feel partly to blame." He moved toward her bedroom door. "I need some fresh air. I'll call you for dinner."

CHAPTER 20

The Sun Deck

"What do you mean, her nephew will get the job? My god, George, are you all a bunch of wimps?" Harriet berated.

Frustrated, their rivalry momentarily cast aside, the group, along with their spouses, had congregated on the sun deck after their shocking meeting with Yvonne.

"We're far from that, Harriet," Jean snapped. "It's easy for you to criticize our behavior. You don't work for the She-Devil."

"Harriet's right," Marge spoke up. "Even though only one of you would have gotten the job, it would at least have been someone who deserved it."

"Take it easy, Marge," her husband urged. "She owns the darn company and, like it or not, we're subject to her whims."

"Whims?" Helen Miller blew up. "Is that what you call her grip on all of you? Whims?"

"From what Simon told me, her nephew's on board," Dina spoke up.

"That's right," Barry finally got a word in. "If he's anything like Yvonne, heaven help us."

"From what I understand, he's no more than a clerk in his uncle's coat factory," Simon reported.

"You mean he has no cosmetics experience? That's ridiculous," Bill said in astonishment.

George sensed the rage that was building in all of them. "Let's look at this objectively. From what Mel told me earlier, the kid is lazy and I'm sure Mel's been trying to convince her to reconsider. In fact, when he left the meeting, he was headed back to their suite to discuss it with her again."

"Fat chance he'll have of convincing her of anything," Harriet exclaimed. "Her heart is as hard as those diamonds she flaunts."

"Maybe one of us should speak to her," Jean suggested.

They were so engrossed in their griping session, they hardly noticed that Taco had joined them and was perched on the railing next to George, who was trying to stay far away from Harriet while he puffed on his favorite walnut blend.

"There you are." Dr. Gordon appeared and called to the bird. "I do hope he hasn't been annoying anyone."

Seizing the break in the controversy, George quickly responded, "No, Doctor. He's been a perfect gentleman. In fact, I believe he's adopted us."

"He does that on every cruise. He takes a liking to one or two passengers and they're his friends for the entire trip," she explained. "He's probably also attracted to the aroma of your tobacco," she added.

"Friends. Taco's friends. Awk."

"Okay, it's time for your lunch now, Taco. I'm sure your friends will understand."

Taco immediately flapped his wings and hopped onto the arm she extended to him. "Time for lunch. Awk."

"Say goodbye."

"Goodbye. Awk."

As spontaneously humorous as his reply was, no one laughed. They just weren't in the mood for levity.

CHAPTER 21

The Infirmary

"Here you go, pretty fellow." The doctor set Taco on his perch and he immediately dipped his beak into his feeding cup.

"He sure does love fruit." Jamie Brewer came into the outer office just as he selected a plump grape.

"I know, but I think it's probably a toss-up between fruit, Taco chips and nuts."

"Speaking of nuts," Nurse Brewer said, "have you noticed the Silvers group? They don't seem to be enjoying themselves very much. None of them have shown any interest in shipboard activities."

"They do stick pretty much together," the doctor observed. "And when I located Taco, he seemed very interested in their discussion. I couldn't help overhearing. It was very heated and they appeared quite agitated."

"Bad lady. Witch. Awk."

"Now stop that, Taco. That's not nice at all," the doctor reprimanded.

"Oh boy, he must have picked that up when he was listening to them." Nurse Brewer shrugged.

"Oh boy. Witch."

"Stop that, Taco."

"Stop that, Taco." He echoed as he bobbed his way across his perch and pulled a choice cashew out of his cup.

CHAPTER 22

The Royal Palm Dining Room

"Well, I'm glad to see Yvonne's bombshell this morning hasn't ruined your appetites," Mel said as he joined the group for dinner.

"And is Yvonne planning a late entrance as usual?" Harriet snipped.

Mel realized he was in for further goading but, in spite of it, right now he preferred their company. "No, I'm sorry to disappoint you," he grinned. "She's dining with her nephew, Stuart, in the Terrace Grill."

"So how'd you get out of it?" Barry asked.

"Yeah?" Dina teased. "How did you manage to slip away?"

"It was Yvonne's decision. It's a family matter she has to deal with, and one I want no part of."

"Good for you, Mel." Jean smiled from across the table.

"Okay," he declared, "how about some champagne? I know you're not in a celebrating mood, but who knows, a lot can change between here and New York."

"You mean you have her reconsidering?" Collin sounded hopeful.

"Not exactly, but there's more than one way to skin a cat." He ordered three bottles of the bubbly.

"I hope you're right, Mel," Harriet exclaimed, "'cause she's one cat I'd love to see skinned."

"Get in line," Marge uttered.

"Ladies, please," Simon scolded. "You're speaking of our leader's wife."

"Perhaps you're going about this in the wrong manner," Jim Dawson interjected as he filled Jean's champagne flute.

"What do you mean?"

"Yeah, Jim?" Collin picked up on his wife's question. "What could we possibly do that would make a difference?"

Mel sat silently listening, knowing he could do little else at this point. Still, he was gratified that they could speak so freely in his presence.

"Well..." Jim started, "perhaps you should approach Mrs. Silvers on a more personal, individual basis. It would seem to me that even a difficult person such as I've been lead to believe... no offense, Mel..."

Mel tipped his glass in a gesture of understanding.

"As I was saying, if each of you were to speak to her explaining your feelings and reminding her of your loyalty to the company, and show her that you realize how difficult it must be for her having to consider a relative over one of you, well... maybe she just needs that kind of understanding. I'm sure it's not easy owning a company and being responsible for so many people and their livelihood."

"You'll have to forgive my husband," Jean apologized. "Running a bookstore clouds one's view of the real world."

"It was just a thought, people," he smirked at her put down.

"Now wait a minute," Simon spoke up. "If you're really interested in getting that job, then I think Jim has a point. I mean, if any of you think you have the leadership qualities to replace Herb, then you should have the gumption to tell Yvonne just how you feel about her choice and let her know how much you really want the position."

"You know, he's right," Barry declared. "Maybe we should go over our feelings on the matter with her one more time."

"Well, George?" Harriet prodded her husband.

"It's a waste of time." He fiddled with his empty pipe. "I'm sure Mel agrees. Once she's made up her mind, she's not likely to change it."

Combing his fingers through his silvery hair, Mel took a moment to compose the right answer. "Knowing how Yvonne reacts to pressure, I'll leave it up to each of you to decide if that's the right course of action."

"In other words, folks," Dina piped in, "approach at your own risk."

Mel nodded at her astute observation. He knew Simon had no interest in the job and that Dina was the aggressive Dumont.

The remainder of their dinner conversation was focused mainly on business ending with Simon inquiring if Yvonne had evaluated the new lip moisturizing cream jar yet.

Mel knew she'd barely glanced at it. "I'm sure she'll get around to it," he replied. "Now, if you'll excuse me, I'll be turning in. I signed up for tomorrow's walking tour of San Juan, so I'd better get a good night's sleep. I hope each of you will find something interesting to do. In the meantime, goodnight, and do enjoy the remainder of the evening." He drained his flute, rose and left them to finish the champagne.

"Since neither of us has ever been to Puerto Rico," Helen said as she also rose to leave, "Barry and I have signed up for the bus tour."

"Beats walking," Barry said as they left the table a few minutes after Mel.

"How about you two?" George addressed Simon and Dina.

"It's the bus for us, also," Simon replied. "There should be some great subject matter along the route."

"Him and his photography," Dina grumbled. "How about the Dawsons and the Collins?" she inquired looking from one to the other.

"We're staying on board and getting a little sun before we reach Aruba," Jean told her.

"Besides," Jim added, "we visited San Juan on our honeymoon."

"It's the bus for us as well," Bill informed them.

"I, for one, have no interest in mingling with the island's poverty," Harriet griped. "Nor do I intend spending my time in some casino watching George make a fool of himself."

"Except I enjoy gaming a little and I usually win, don't I, dear?" George insisted.

"Suit yourself."

Just to rub a little salt, Jean mentioned that Yvonne was staying on board as well.

"Maybe you two can get a massage together," she suggested to Harriet.

"Only if they can rub some of the meanness out of her," Harriet shot back.

"I'll be glad to help," Helen offered.

"Looks like this dinner's over," Simon observed.

CHAPTER 23

The Terrace Grill

An intimate dining room, the Terrace Grill accommodated only a few dozen passengers. The menu was more limited than the larger dining room and most of the tables were set up for couples. Soft lighting, velour seating, plush carpeting and the gentle piano tempo of Gershwin enhanced the romantic ambiance of the room. It was the ideal atmosphere for a private talk, especially the chat that was taking place at a certain corner table.

"I purposely kept your presence on board confidential until after we'd had this little talk, Stuart."

"I suppose, Aunt Yvonne, that explains the inconvenient accommodations I'm putting up with on C-deck."

Except for the slight stutter that had plagued him since childhood, he was much like his father with the same red face and pudgy build.

He listened as she continued. "Let's not get off to a negative beginning, Stuart. Sometimes there's a reason for such caution in the business world. I would have hoped your Uncle Abe had taught you as much…"

"There's no backstabbing on my mother's side of the family. We have no need to sneak around and hide what we're doing. Besides, the coat business is not like selling false hope to ugly women," he blurted out.

"Maybe your Uncle Mel is right. You do have a superior attitude, especially toward women," she continued. "I want you to pay attention now, young man, because I'm trying very hard to discuss an opportunity for you to become more than a rag peddler. The least you can do is hear me out. If you consider my offer carefully, I'm sure you'll realize how much it could mean to you."

Their waiter approached. "May I get you something from the bar?" he offered.

"Yeah. I'll have a Bloody Mary." Stuart ordered without looking at the man.

"And you, Madam?"

"Just some ice water."

He left menus and proceeded to get their drinks. As soon he was out of earshot, Stuart fired back, "Like the opportunity you gave my father?"

Seeming to ignore the dig, Yvonne went on. "Myron and I had a misunderstanding. This discussion has nothing to do with that."

"Oh sure." He cut it short as their drinks arrived. After taking a quick swig, he asked, "And where's poor Uncle Mel? Does he know I'm on board?"

"Of course he does. He's dining with some of our employees. I made it clear that this is a family matter and that I wished to meet with you alone."

He watched her roll the cold glass between her palms. "I see you're still treating him like a lap dog. What's the matter, Auntie? Isn't Uncle Mel heeling anymore?"

"That's enough of your wise mouth, Stuart. I asked you to join me on this trip to discuss your future. Why can't you be civil for once?"

He took another gulp, then said, "You know how I feel regarding wha-a-t you did to my father, and until that's settled..." He struggled to control his stutter.

"That's what I'm trying to tell you, for heaven sakes. I know Myron disagreed with how I invested our inheritance, and now I'm trying to make amends, even though I know what I did was right."

"You kept him out of your plans completely and that hurt him more than just financially."

"I did give him his share of…"

"Sure, after you established your own success. If it weren't for his sensitivity, he would have dragged you through the courts. Believe me, Mom urged him to do it ma-ma-ny times. After Father died, she kept insisting that I pursue it right up until her death. So you see, Auntie, bitterness is inbred in me."

"I was very sorry when Esther passed away, Stuart. Although we differed in many ways, I did appreciate how much she loved Myron. That's why I want you to accept my offer and become my Senior Vice President and General Manager. The salary and stock options will more than compensate for any bad feelings you still have."

The conversation stopped while the waiter served their first course.

"That's quite an offer, Auntie." It was obvious that she was doing this to draw him in and avoid any bad press a possible family lawsuit would create. When she had ultimately settled up with his father, one of the stipulations had been that since she and Mel were childless, Stuart would inherit twenty-five percent of the business. That agreement had kept his father from pursuing legal action. Stuart was aware, however, that she still considered him a threat to her and he planned to make the most of it.

"Well, you don't seem too excited about the opportunity to work for the third largest cosmetics company in the States," she said as she attacked her salad.

"Mystified would be a more accurate description." He bit into a huge shrimp. "What's the catch, Auntie? There must be more to this than your benevolence."

"Only that if you accept, you must give complete loyalty to Silvers and to me personally." Looking down at her plate, she said loudly, "Those idiots in the kitchen overcooked my lamb chop." She signaled for their waiter.

Stuart suspected, if he accepted the job, her feigned generosity would be just another way of exploiting his family. "I'll need some time to think about this, Aunt Yvonne."

"Bring me a properly cooked lamb chop, and I don't wish to spend the entire cruise waiting for it," she chastised the waiter.

"Yes, ma'am."

Stuart watched as the frustrated waiter grabbed her plate and dashed back to the kitchen. He realized that working for her would make him as humble as she had just made that poor waiter. His animosity toward her was growing stronger by the minute and he now knew exactly what he had to do. This trip and her underhanded, self-serving, attempted manipulation of him had brought it all into focus.

"All right, Stuart, I understand there's a lot for you to consider. Why don't you join me, along with Mel and the people who would be working for you, at dinner tomorrow evening? After that you can give me your decision."

Their waiter returned with her dinner.

"It still looks overdone," she complained as he stood by anticipating her approval, "but I'll manage in spite of it." She waved him off with her fork as she sliced into the lamb chop.

Stuart could feel the waiter's resentment melding with his own as he faced the vicious person sitting across from him.

"Tomorrow evening sounds fine, Aunt Yvonne." He concentrated on his filet that was done to perfection.

CHAPTER 24

Port of San Juan

It was eight-thirty and all passengers who were disembarking were ready for a full day in San Juan.

"Ladies and gentlemen, those of you who signed up for the bus tour, please meet Nurse Jamie Brewer, our Activities Director, at the end of the pier where she will escort you to the bus. For those of you on the walking tour, Nurse Brewer will introduce you to your local guide. All others who are freewheeling for the day will find a map of the city, along with a lunch chit, in your shore-fun envelope distributed during breakfast. Do enjoy your day, and remember we leave port at precisely six p.m. with no exceptions. So please arrive back here on time."

Taco was perched on a side rail near Ken Boslow during his announcement. As the day-trippers filed off the ship he repeated, "Be back on time. Awk."

Those of the Silvers group who were going ashore parted company at the end of the pier.

Mel, in his neat Brooks Brothers short set, walking shoes and a brimmed straw hat, strode off with half a dozen other exercise enthusiasts.

The Dumonts, Collins and Millers boarded a blue bus and waved to George who was flagging a taxi.

*   *   *

"Did shore leave go well, Ken?" Captain Markem approached the purser soon after the last passenger had disembarked.

"Yes, sir, a total of fifty-six passengers are ashore," Boslow reported.

"Fifty-six, Captain. Awk." As usual, Taco had been paying close attention, and his presence at any given time was an accepted fact.

"That's right, Taco. And we're taking on seven additional passengers today. Is that correct, Ken?"

"Seven more," echoed Taco.

"Yes, sir. I believe they're mostly local insurance agents."

"Very well." With no passengers nearby, the captain lit a cigar and puffed down wind. "Let me know when to welcome the new arrivals."

"Yes sir. They'll probably board sporadically during the day. I'll let you know when they're all checked in."

Dr. Gordon joined them. "Hi, Captain. Ken. Has Taco been behaving himself?"

"Oh, he's been keeping a close tally of our passengers," Boslow replied.

"Close tally," added Taco.

Ignoring the parrot, the captain asked, "Are you going ashore, Gwen?" He stopped puffing as he spoke.

"Yes, I'm looking up an old friend from the Jersey City police force. He and his wife have a time-share down here and they invited me to visit. Besides, I need a little solid ground under my feet, I'm still not as seaworthy as you old salts."

"Old salts. Awk."

"That's enough out of you, Taco. Now you behave while I'm gone."

"Behave. Awk." Taco flapped his wings, flew down onto the deck, and waddled away repeating, "Behave. Taco behave."

"That's one smart parrot," the captain commented as he walked off in the opposite direction in a small cloud of blue smoke.

"Sometimes I think he's a little too smart," the doctor quipped as she headed down the gangplank.

CHAPTER 25

The Ship's Beauty Salon

Jean was having her nails done when Harriet entered the salon. "So you decided against a massage with Her Highness," she teased.

"I have no idea what she's up to today and I could care less. The last I saw of her, she and Mel were having breakfast alone."

Tones of soft pink velour wall covering, matching seating and workstations, complemented by shades of blue linens, carpeting and staff uniforms, clearly achieved the feminine character the salon decorator wished to achieve.

Normally the two operators easily handled a half-dozen pampered women at a time; however, only three chairs were currently occupied.

"What can we do for you today, Madam?" a uniformed operator addressed Harriet.

"I'd like a wash and blow dry," Harriet replied as she took the seat the young stylist indicated. Turning, she said to Jean, "This is the way I like it, no waiting."

"That's what I said when I came in and they told me that since we are in port with so few passengers left aboard, no appointment is needed."

"And what's Jim up to?"

"He's somewhere on the Sun Deck reading. He brought a couple of new novels along. You'd think, after spending his days in a bookstore, he'd take a break from books, but not Jim."

"Some people are totally immersed in their area of interest," Harriet replied as her hair was being washed. "It's like George with his cards and pipe smoking; they both annoy the heck out of me and he seems to enjoy them even more because they do."

Jean's nails were done. "Okay, I'm off to find my enlightened mate and maybe take a swim. Why don't you join us for lunch on the Lido Deck?"

"Thanks, I will," Harriet accepted as the stylist applied setting gel and began working with a hand-held dryer and brush arranging her hair in the bouffant style she preferred.

CHAPTER 26

Old San Juan

Dr. Gordon waved for a taxi when she got to the Tourism Company Center at the end of the Cruise Ship Pier 1 where the Coral Queen was docked. "Calle San Miguel," she instructed the driver. "I believe it's number 72."

The aging cab's air conditioning consisted of open windows that filled the car with city heat. Nevertheless, Dr. Gordon smiled as she recalled that her brother had once owned the same model and year Chevy Bel Air. The route the driver took was directly up Calle De San Justo that ran through the heart of Old San Juan. She figured he had taken this route where they encountered heavy traffic - a stoplight at almost every intersection, and masses of tourists crowding the streets and narrow sidewalks - to add to the metered fare. Her instincts as a retired cop almost caused her to chew him out for taking advantage of yet another tourist, but she had to admit it was a pleasant ride and the storefronts and antiquated structures did have an old world charm and calming effect. Besides, being on land was a welcome diversion.

Her thoughts were interrupted when the driver slowed to a stop, "Very nice jewelry and watches inside, Lady. Would you like to see?"

"No, driver, just take me to the address I gave you."

"Sí, Calle San Miguel, but if you would care to buy something I will be glad to wait, and my cousin, Hector, will give you a very nice price."

Slightly annoyed, Dr. Gordon opened her door and feigned getting out. "I guess I'll just get another taxi," she threatened.

"No, no, Lady, please, we will go now."

"Are you sure we won't disappoint Hector?" she scoffed holding the door partly open.

"Sí, Lady, sí."

She closed the heavy door and he peeled away.

*   *   *

Seventy-two Calle San Miguel was a nine-story pink stucco high-rise with balconies that overlooked the Atlantic.

Ed Brody greeted Gwen moments after she pressed the buzzer of Apartment 712.

"Gwen," he shouted. "It's good to see you. When you called last night, Sally and I were so pleased to hear from you and we're glad you found time to visit us."

She was hardly inside when the huge man unexpectedly grabbed and hugged her. "Likewise, Ed," she gulped.

"Sally's in the kitchen, she'll…"

"Ed, don't crush the poor woman. Hi," she greeted Gwen when he released her. "I'm Sally, and I'm very happy to meet you, Doctor. Ed mentioned you a lot when he was still on the force."

"Hi, Sally. Now I remember what a big huggy bear he always was. And please call me Gwen," she said as she handed Sally a bottle of wine from the ship, then adjusted the street clothes she was wearing for the day.

"It's a habit I can't seem to break him of," she gave Ed a fake punch on his biceps.

"Except when I hug her," he teased.

It was happy couples like the Brodys that caused Dr. Gordon to sometimes regret that she had never married. But after years of studying, practicing medicine and then forensic police work, there had never been any space on her dance card for a partner. Unfortunately, life on a cruise ship hadn't broadened the prospects, at least not yet.

"Let's sit on the balcony, Gwen, I made some iced tea, or shall I open the wine?" Sally asked as she led the way.

"Tea will be fine, thanks." Gwen studied the condo as they passed through the living room. Even though she had never been in a time-share apartment, the décor and furnishing were as simple and functional as she would have imagined.

"I'd like something stronger," Ed replied.

"I'll put an extra cube in your tea," Sally offered.

Like the interior accommodations, the sturdy plastic chairs and table on the balcony appeared to be built to withstand repeated use.

"The view of the Atlantic from land is quite different from the view you get aboard ship," Gwen commented as they sat together sipping tea. It was a balmy morning. Not a single cloud marred the clear blue sky. She could, however, feel a slight breeze, the benefit of being on the seventh floor.

"What about your new job, Gwen?" Ed asked as he reclined on a lounge that wasn't built for his size. "We were all surprised to learn that you were working on a cruise ship after you resigned from our forensics department."

"It must be exotic," Sally remarked. "I mean traveling from port to port and meeting so many interesting people,"

"So far it's been fun and I like the other crew members I work with."

"She means available bachelors," Ed chided. "Sally's a real romantic type. I keep telling her she reads too many novels."

"Ignore him, Gwen. It wouldn't hurt you to read more, Mr. Smart Pants."

"I did enough reading when I was on the force, only that stuff was real."

"From that standpoint, Ed's right, Sally. It's the reason I packed it in early. Too much violence and long, thankless hours." She reached over and poured herself more tea.

"I'm glad Ed's time was up. He's a different person now. I could always sense the strain he was under as a homicide detective."

"That's right, Doc," he addressed her as he had back then. "Now all we do is travel to a couple of time-shares and visit our kids who live in North Carolina and Connecticut. It sure beats traveling from one crime scene to another." He looked at his watch. "How about lunch? There's a great little seafood grill just down the avenue." He got up and stretched his six-foot-four frame.

"Or if you prefer, Gwen, I could make some sandwiches here."

"Don't bother, Sally, the seafood grill will be fine."

*   *   *

Ed was right, the grill had a good selection of fresh local catches and the wine he insisted on ordering complemented their choices. Sally suggested they sit outside rather than in the chilly interior of the restaurant. She made the point that if you came to the islands to enjoy the weather, then you should enjoy it, not hide from it inside where the air is conditioned.

Dr. Gordon agreed with her. Shaded by a huge green umbrella, they found the view across the road to the ocean to be delightful. Bathers on the beach and vessels beyond the surf completed the tranquil scene.

By the time they finished a leisurely lunch and talked about old times and some of the tough cases they had worked on together, it was getting close to three o-clock. Gwen had planned to do a little personal shopping before re-boarding and now her time was running short. When the check came, she beat Ed to it.

"You're supposed to be our guest." He tried reaching for the chit but she held it out of his long reach.

"He's right, Gwen. It is our treat."

"Tell you what then, Brodys, I'll be back this way when you're down here again and I'll let you treat me. How's that?' she suggested as she held out the check and a credit card for the young waitress who had served them.

When they parted in front of the grill, Ed gave her another bear hug.

"Please remember to visit again, Gwen." Sally said as she gave her a peck on the cheek.

"I will, I promise."

"And Doc, if you're ever in North Jersey in June or December, be sure to look us up." He placed his arm around Sally's waist while they waited for her to flag a taxi.

*   *   *

Quickly completing her shopping errands, Dr. Gordon returned to the ship an hour prior to the first back-on-board warning blasts. Returning to her quarters next to the infirmary, she came across Taco on the arm of a one of the dining room chefs.

"Welcome aboard, Doc. Awk."

"I can see you didn't miss me very much," she answered him. "Hi, Carlo, has he been a pest while I was gone?"

"Nah. We don't get to see our little friend too often," Carlo told her as he fed Taco a crisp cracker.

"That's 'cause the kitchens and dining rooms are off limits to him." She held out her arm and Taco hopped onto it.

"Off limits," Taco repeated.

"Thanks, Carlo. See you later." She took the remaining cracker he handed her.

"Thanks, Carlo. Awk."

"You're welcome, funny bird." Carlo headed down the corridor to the crew's quarters laughing as Dr. Gordon and Taco entered her cabin.

An hour later she was awakened from a short nap by the blast of the ship's final boarding reminder.

CHAPTER 27

The Sun Deck

"Here come the bus people now," Jean remarked. She, Jim and Harriet were enjoying early evening drinks on the sun deck.

The Millers, Collins and Dumonts joined them and promptly ordered from the bar waiter.

Flopping onto a nearby lounge, Dina stretched her legs, kicked off her flats and complained, "Some bus ride if you call walking all over Old San Juan, through El Morro Castle and every other jewelry store on the island a bus ride."

"You need more exercise, Dear," Simon teased as he snapped a shot of his wife rubbing her feet.

"I get plenty at home, and enough with the camera." She tossed a shoe at him.

Shielding his treasured Nikon, he caught it in midair.

"Nice catch," Barry said as he accepted his drink from the waiter.

"I must say, they could have done a better job of keeping the bus clean," Marge griped. "Did you see all those empty cups and discarded burger wrappers under some of the seats?"

"I only saw one cup, Marge," Bill corrected her, "and it may have been put there by one of our fellow passengers."

Jean Dawson glanced over at Helen and they both smirked.

Harriet wasn't all that amused by any of their remarks. She pretended to ignore them while she kept looking down the deck for George. She knew he had gone off to gamble at one of the local hotel casinos. It was one of his stupid diversions that she hated and she planned to remind him of it again this evening. "Have any of you seen George or Mel?" she asked checking her watch.

"Mel arrived when we did," Barry told her. "He went straight to his cabin. Said he was going to take a well-earned shower."

"He's in pretty good shape," Helen observed. "He told me they walked through Old San Juan and all the way back to the pier."

"That's some hike," Simon agreed.

"What about George?" Harriet insisted expecting someone to reply.

"Haven't seen him since we left this morning," Barry told her and the others said the same.

"I'll bet he lost again and has gone straight to our room. See you all at dinner." Harriet swung off her lounge and proceeded toward their suite.

Before she was out of sight, they heard her exclaim, "Move, you dumb parrot."

"Dumb parrot," Taco mimicked as he waddled over to the group and perched on the arm of Jim's lounge.

"Okay, Taco, hold it." Simon focused on the bird as the glow of sunset gave everything on the sun deck a warm orange cast. "My last shot of the day," he declared as he snapped the shutter.

"Thank goodness," Dina sighed. "Now put your toy away and let's go get ready for dinner."

"I guess it's time for us to depart, too." Barry and Helen headed off.

"Poor George," Jean said sympathetically. "I'm afraid he's in for it when Harriet catches up with him." She gathered up her sandals and slipped them back on.

"Party's over. little guy," Jim said.

"Party's over," Taco repeated to his departing friends.

CHAPTER 28

The Bridge of the Coral Queen

"Captain, we have a problem," Ken Boslow called Capt. Markem on the bridge where he was busy navigating the ship into open water.

"Oh? What's that, Ken?"

"It's Mrs. Porter. She's with the cosmetics company group."

"Hold on, Ken." Markem gave the helmsman corrective directions. "Okay, Ken, what is it now?"

"It appears Mr. Porter didn't make it back to the ship on time."

"Oh, no!" Knowing how precise his purser always was, Markem felt uneasy asking if he had checked the return roster. "Are you certain? Maybe he's…"

"Yes, sir, I'm certain. We double-checked. And, according to procedure, we sounded the return-to-ship horn three times at half-hour intervals prior to departure. Of the fifty-six passengers who went ashore this morning, only fifty-five have returned, plus the seven new passengers who joined us here in San Juan. They're all berthed on C deck."

"Fine. I'll greet them during dinner. Now, are you sure it's her husband who didn't re-board?"

"He phoned her, said he had been gambling in the Sea Breeze Casino all afternoon, lost track of time and didn't hear the ship's warning horns. She's insisting we turn around."

Capt. Markem looked out toward the receding shoreline. Taking off his cap he ran his fingers through his hair as he considered the problem George Porter's negligence had created. There was no way they could turn back and he was grateful most passengers respected their timetables, though one did occasionally miss the boat.

"Tell her we can't do that. We've already cleared the harbor."

"I told her that, Captain, and reminded her that in your welcome aboard instructions, you explained the strict company rule that the ship must stay on schedule with no exceptions. Nevertheless, she's very agitated and wants to speak to you, Sir."

"All right, Ken, try to keep her calm. Tell Mrs. Porter I'll join you and her in the off deck lounge as soon as possible."

"Yes, Sir."

Markem then studied the ship's position, giving the helmsman further instructions as they sailed into open water.

*   *   *

"He's an idiot," Harriet screeched.

Capt. Markem could see he was dealing with an unreasonable woman, but he nodded and smiled his most accommodating smile. As Captain, he was obliged to pacify passengers like her.

"And I don't see why you couldn't have waited for him, Captain. George claims he was on the dock when we pulled away."

None of them realized that Taco was perched nearby, until he squawked, "George missed the boat."

"I don't find that stupid bird amusing under the circumstances, Captain," Harriet snapped, her anger obviously out of control.

"Ken, perhaps Taco shouldn't be here right now." The captain made a discreet gesture toward the door.

Boslow gently urged Taco onto his forearm, carried him out and then returned.

"Well, Captain, what do I do now?" Harriet fumed.

"We've had this happen once or twice before, Mrs. Porter," Capt. Markem assured her. "The usual procedure when a passenger misses the boat is they book a room for the night and the next day take a flight to our next port of call, which in this case will be Aruba."

"You'll see, Mrs. Porter," Boslow added a little more reassurance, "he'll be fine."

Apparently unconvinced, Harriet continued her tirade. "Humph. Knowing George, he'll be up half the night with his pipe in one hand and playing cards in the other."

"May I escort you back to your cabin?" Boslow offered.

"No, thanks." She headed out the door where she was again greeted by Taco.

"Awk. Miss George."

"You're the only one who does, you dumb parrot," Harriet growled as she steamed off looking for the nearest martini.

"Dumb parrot," Taco mimicked her growl as she disappeared into the small bar on the top deck.

CHAPTER 29

Executive Suite 1B

"I don't see what pleasure you could have gotten from roaming around those filthy streets in all this heat," Yvonne chided as Mel stripped off his walking outfit.

Still wearing his damp shorts, Mel tossed his sweaty shirt into a nearby laundry hamper, then faced his wife and replied, "San Juan is a beautiful city, Yvonne, and it's a heck of a lot cleaner than some parts of New York. Besides, the exercise was invigorating and good for me. You should have joined us."

"Not on your life. Go wash up before you smell up the entire cabin."

He flapped his arms in a fanning motion as he headed for a refreshing shower.

As he adjusted the water temperature, he yelled, "I left so early this morning that you were still asleep and we didn't have a chance to talk about your discussion with Stuart last night. How'd it go?"

Not about to give him the satisfaction of knowing how disturbing the evening with her nasty nephew had been, Yvonne shouted back, "I'll tell you later. He's joining us for dinner this evening. The little ingrate reacted just as I thought he would. As an officer of the company, he would then have no legal grounds for a lawsuit, but if he pursues that course, I'll change my will regardless of what I promised Myron. One way or the other, I'll not be forced to relinquish any part of what I've worked so hard to create."

While she waited for Mel, Yvonne flipped through several evening dresses in her closet, then opened the room safe and toyed with her jewelry trying to decide which piece went best with the dress she had chosen.

CHAPTER 30

The Royal Palm Dining Room

"The darn fool missed the boat." Harriet gulped her before-dinner martini with more than her usual relish as though it would lessen her anger over George's stupidity, while she explained his absence to most of the group already seated for dinner. "Him and his blackjack!" She licked the brim of her glass. "Wouldn't you think that dumb casino would alert players when a ship is ready to leave?"

"Poor George," Barry declared as the Millers arrived at the table.

"We just heard," Helen remarked, then added, "I see Yvonne and Mel haven't shown up yet. Do they know about George?"

"Late entrance as usual," Jean declared. "I'm sure George's not being here won't matter a bit to her... sorry, Harriet."

Draining her glass, Harriet restated, "He's a fool." She signaled for another drink.

"Poor George is right," Bill Collin whispered to Marge. "I pity him when he gets back on board."

"Bill!" his wife cautioned.

*   *   *

Stuart saw the group and hesitated to approach them when he didn't see either Mel or Yvonne among them. After all, he had no idea what she might have told them about him or how they would react to his appearance at their table. He hoped they would understand that this was all Yvonne's idea and that he was as much at her mercy as they were, except that he could still say yes or no and they were already in her employ.

When he realized they were watching him, it was too late for him to silently turn away. "Hi," he finally greeted them. "I understand this is the Silvers' table."

"Yes, you must be Yvonne's nephew." Simon stood and introduced himself. The others remained seated.

"That's right, I'm Stuart Rosen." Stuart grasped the hand Simon offered as if grabbing for a life preserver. "I see, being true to form, my aunt and Mel are fashionably late," he added with a tentative grin.

"A privilege they apparently enjoy," Simon replied. "Let me introduce everyone."

As soon as the intros were complete, Harriet pointed to the empty chair next to her. "You might as well take this seat, Stuart, George missed the boat."

Stuart looked perplexed as he sat in the chair she indicated.

Barry quickly explained adding, "Her husband, George, is VP of our R&D Operations."

"I see you've all managed to meet and welcome Stuart," Mel said to the group as he held Yvonne's chair when they finally arrived.

Yvonne had selected a perfect pear cut, six-carat diamond pendant for the evening. It fit snugly into the scooped neckline of her silk evening dress. The simplicity of the platinum chain and setting enhanced the beauty of the stone.

"Good to see you, Uncle Mel." Stuart rose and shook his uncle's hand. "Aunt Yvonne," he nodded. It was an obviously cool greeting as he meant it to be. Grasping her limp hand, he discreetly passed her a note.

Palming the missive for a moment, Yvonne scanned the table. "Where is George, our illustrious researcher?"

On her second martini, Harriet simply replied,"He's lost."

Since Harriet appeared to be engrossed in her martini, Jean took it upon herself to explain George's absence.

"Rather careless behavior, the fool," Yvonne remarked. Interrupted by the waiter taking her dinner order, she tucked the note into her evening bag.

Stuart enjoyed the intolerant look on her face as she stared directly at him. He simply smiled back at her. Until later, Auntie, he thought.

"Now don't you dare interrupt me," she warned Mel as she was about to address the group. As if she didn't already have their full attention, Yvonne tapped a spoon against her water glass. "As I told you on our first night out," she placed her hand on Mel's shoulder, "we are considering my nephew, Stuart, for the position of Senior VP…"

The clank of a dropped fork hitting a dish interrupted her little spiel.

"Sorry, Yvonne," Simon apologized.

"I hope you hold your crayons firmer than that, you clumsy Frenchman. As for the rest of you, please hang onto your silverware until I'm finished," she barked as she stared at each of them.

"Yvonne!" Mel scolded.

Stuart watched this little tirade, shocked but not at all surprised at the audacity of the woman. He could see the pain and hatred in their eyes as she tormented them in the presence of their spouses who looked at her with equal contempt. If looks could kill, Auntie, you'd be dead several times over.

"As I was saying, Stuart and I had a brief discussion last evening and I'm still convinced that he's the best candidate for the job." With a disingenuous smile, she peered directly at her nephew, then went on. "I know you're thinking he's a bit young, but he's a Rosen, and Mel and I will guide his every move. So that's it, and until it's official, keep your petty disappointments to yourselves. Do I make myself clear?"

Stuart was about to comment but the flushed expressions of disgust surrounding him prevented him from causing a scene. There are better ways to deal with this witch.

Instead, he offered a toast, "To the success of Silvers, whoever may be in charge."

Waiters serving dinner interrupted their insincere response of raised glasses.

Thereafter, except for Harriet's slurred bemoaning of George's absence, small talk was at a minimum during the meal.

As soon as coffee arrived, Stuart watched Yvonne unfold and read his note.

After giving him another stern look, Yvonne stood. "I believe I'll get some air, Mel."

"You go ahead, I'd like a cognac after my coffee," he replied. "I'll see you back in our suite later."

"Suit yourself. Stuart, would you please join me?" It was more of a command than an invitation.

"Sure, Aunt Yvonne." He was hoping to unload what was on his mind and the sooner he let her have it, the better. He bid them all a good evening and joined her as she turned her back and left the table.

*   *   *

Although the night sky was overcast, the evening sea was illuminated by the ship's brilliant glow. As they walked along the quiet deck, Stuart fantasized his aunt falling into that beautiful, deep, shimmering ocean.

Her shrill voice broke the illusion. "Just what is this dumb note all about?" She shook it in his face, then crumpled it and tossed it down onto the deck. "How dare you. You must never play games with me, young man. You're being stupid and childish avoiding what I'm offering you."

The sound of music came from a small bar lounge they were passing. "Let's go inside, Auntie, and have a drink."

"All right, but I warn you, this is the last discussion on the subject."

Inside the bar an old-time Wurlitzer juke box with bubbling lights was playing bee-bop tunes.

"There," Stuart pointed. "There's space over there." He led the way to an unoccupied table near a window.

A number of the insurance group who were also on board stared as Yvonne and Stuart made their way across the room. At first Stuart thought it might be their age difference that caused the glances. Then he realized it was the jumbo chunk of sparkle hanging around his aunt's neck that had caught their eyes. A $100,000 diamond would certainly draw anyone's attention, especially insurance agents.

The lounge was decorated in a fifties motif. Large photo-murals of Cadillacs, Chevys and Fords with piercing tail fins covered the walls. Mock auto headlights illuminated the bar area and red plastic taillights glowed from each of the dozen or so tables. The single waitress wore a poodle skirt and saddle shoes.

Yvonne looked around. "Hurry and order. This place is horrid," she grumbled as her face twisted into an impatient grimace.

"What's wrong, Auntie, weren't the fifties kind to you?" He was enjoying her discomfort. He had despised this woman ever since he was a small boy and now she was trying to entice him to become her employee.

"Hi, what'll it be, folks?" the waitress asked as she twirled her poodle skirt.

"A brandy for the lady and a bottle of champagne. And we're in kind of a hurry." He was keyed up and anxious to get this encounter over with.

"A big hurry." Yvonne's voice was both demanding and demeaning.

The music was loud enough to muffle their conversation so Stuart spoke freely.

"How can you treat people the way you do?" He unconsciously pressed his hands together tightly.

"I treat everyone equally, which does have its advantages. Did you see how fast we got our drinks?" Yvonne sipped her brandy and glanced about the room as Stuart uncorked the champagne. "Horrible little lounge, but their bar stock is premium quality." She turned and faced him. "Now, forget your feelings toward me and think of your future. Will you reconsider or not? I'd like to take my evening walk before retiring." She yawned in his face.

"I feel sorry for those poor saps who work for you, Auntie. I don't see how you could possibly believe that I would become one of them."

She fingered her diamond possessively. "I should have expected as much from you. It doesn't surprise me that you're weak. You're just like your father."

"Not quite." He wasn't about to allow her to see how much she riled him.

"Since you've made your decision perfectly clear, I'll just finish my brandy and leave you to stew in your own misery." She took several more swallows, drained her glass, rose and said, "Good night, and remember, you'll live to regret your ingratitude and the opportunity you're throwing away. Enjoy the remainder of your free cruise."

"I will, Auntie." He didn't get up, just tilted his flute. "In fact, I'm going to sit here and enjoy the fifties. Have a good long sleep."

He watched her leave and once again her diamond necklace drew stares as she departed.

*   *   *

"That dumb, ignorant, little fool, I'll grind him into the ground." She was quietly spouting off into the night as she walked in the direction of the dining room to find Mel. He'll only say he was right all along. With that unpleasant thought, she turned and headed for their suite.

Suddenly, Taco startled her as he imitated her tone of voice and her last words. "Grind him into the ground. Awk." He was sitting on the railing just ahead of her.

"Stupid bird, you should be in a cage," she exclaimed as she strode toward him, making a mental note to complain to the cruise line regarding pesky, annoying animals allowed to roam freely about the ship.

Had she not rushed past him so quickly, she might have heard Taco's subsequent greeting to someone following her. Seconds later, Yvonne heard footsteps and became aware that she was not alone on that dark, deserted section of the deck. She gripped her diamond pendant, and quickened her pace toward her cabin. The footsteps became louder and louder until whoever had been following behind overtook and passed her, then abruptly turned and confronted her. Suddenly she was face to face with the other late night stroller.

"You! I don't understand…"

"It doesn't matter what you understand or think anymore."

"Get out of my way. I've no time for your games." She pushed forward in an attempt to get by and reach her cabin.

A sudden, severe blow to her head stopped her. The lethal sounds of crushed skull bones and a bottle cracking disrupted the serenity of the warm evening. The force of the impact twisted Yvonne around and she slumped backwards over the ship's railing.

For a few short seconds, her quivering body dangled there. Then Taco, a short distance farther down the deck, watched as Yvonne's legs were lifted and she was tilted over the side. Still holding the cracked champagne bottle by its neck, Yvonne's assailant started to move away from the railing where she had gone over, then instinctively turned and flung the bottle toward the sea. Quickly running away into the silent night, the assailant unknowingly dropped something.

"Man overboard. Awk, man overboard," Taco squawked, but no one heard him. A few minutes later the parrot flew down onto the deck, waddled over, retrieved the dropped object and headed back to his perch in the infirmary.

*   *   *

It was after midnight when Mel returned to their suite, and prepared for bed. Buttoning his pajama shirt, he stared out the window into the dark sea. His brain was fuzzy from too much to drink and everything that had transpired earlier.

Just before turning off his light, he took a couple of aspirins. Then opening his closet, he removed the walking outfit and shoes he intended to wear the following morning in Aruba. He climbed into bed and was soon asleep.

CHAPTER 31

Port of Aruba

"There you all are. Ready for a great day ashore?" Mel greeted his group as he joined them at the buffet breakfast.

"It's a beautiful day for it." Jean indicated the empty seat between her and Harriet Porter.

"Thanks, Jean," he said sitting between the two women.

Their table overlooked Cruise Ship Pier 9 where they had just docked. Simon took full advantage of the view, snapping one interesting shot after another of the shore activities below.

Mel turned to Harriet, "I guess we'll be getting George back today."

"Yes. And I'm staying on board to be sure he stays put this time and doesn't get left behind again." She mashed a pat of butter onto a roll.

"Another walking tour, Mel?" Bill Collin changed the subject.

"Absolutely." Mel reached for the coffee carafe and poured the much needed steaming brew into his cup. "I find it both invigorating and relaxing. I just wish I could convince Yvonne to join me. I keep telling her the exercise does wonders."

"So, why doesn't she? It's certainly good for the figure." Dina's dig didn't go unnoticed.

Mel took a big swallow of his coffee before replying. "Yvonne likes to sleep in, and I've learned the hard way to let her." He added more cream to his coffee and reached for a croissant.

"So, Mel, what's the decision on Stuart?" Barry asked loud enough for the others to hear.

"She won't budge," Mel replied.

Ken Boslow's voice came over the loudspeaker. "All passengers going ashore please proceed to the upper deck."

"I guess that means us," Simon said as he took a final photo of some men securing a rope to the ship.

Just as they were finishing, Stuart joined them. "It's a great day. I think I'll walk with you, Uncle Mel," he announced.

*   *   *

Twenty minutes later, they were in line waiting to disembark.

"Enjoy your day," Pursor Boslow announced as the gangplank was being affixed to the ship, "and please," he emphasized loudly, "remember to listen for the warning signals for re-boarding."

"Warning signals," Taco added as he perched on the railing near Boslow. "Warning signals," he repeated as several people walked past him.

"We will," one of the passengers laughingly replied.

Scanning the dock, Bill asked, "Does anyone see George?"

"I don't see him, and I'm afraid he's in for it when he does show up," Mel commented as he headed off with Stuart for their walking tour.

"Poor George," Simon agreed as he snapped a shot of Jean in a big-brimmed straw hat before they all parted to go their separate ways and engage in their chosen activities for the day.

Nurse Brewer greeted them on the pier. She handed out lunch chits and street maps of Oranjistad. "You're on your own today," she announced. "The orange busses are for our ship's passengers and will return here on time. Now all you free-wheelers have fun and watch the clock." She left them and re-boarded the ship.

*   *   *

Two hours after the day-trippers had left the ship, Roger Wills sought out the captain. Spotting him chatting with an older couple at the breakfast bar, Wills approached as discreetly as possible.

"Captain, if I might have a word with you, Sir," he nervously interrupted.

Seeing the look of distress in his First Mate's eyes, Markem smiled and politely excused himself. "Duty calls." He could see that Wills was barely able to contain himself.

When they were completely out of earshot, Wills exclaimed, "John." He only used the captain's name when they were alone. "A member of the crew found a dead woman in one of the lower deck lifeboats."

"What? How?"

"He noticed that the cover tie-downs were broken and the canvas was pulled into the boat. When he climbed up to fix it, there she was."

As they made their way to the lower deck, Markem asked, "Are you sure she's dead? Have you contacted Gwen?"

"Yes. Dr. Gordon should be down there by now. I've no doubt she's dead from what I could see."

With no passengers in sight, they picked up their pace. Approaching the scene, they found Nurse Brewer standing on deck next to a crewman who was supporting a ladder leading up the side of the lifeboat.

"Gwen's up there, Captain," Nurse Brewer informed him when they reached the boat.

Markem paced the area impatiently looking up from time to time awaiting word from the doctor. He unbuttoned his jacket and loosened his tie. When he could no longer contain his anxiety, he reached for a rung of the ladder. He was about to go up when Dr. Gordon's head appeared over the edge.

"No point in making the climb, Captain. She's dead all right, and it looks like it wasn't an accident."

"Just what does that mean?" He stepped aside as the doctor climbed down and joined him back on deck.

"Here, Wills, this obviously broke loose when she hit. You'd better hang on to it." Dr. Gordon handed Yvonne's diamond necklace to the First Mate who was also the ship's security officer.

After examining the huge stone, Wills slipped it into his jacket pocket.

Dr. Gordon again faced the captain. "It means, John, she was murdered by a sharp blow to her frontal lobe area. In other words, someone bashed in her head with a heavy, blunt object. Judging from her evening dress and that rock she's wearing, it happened during the night. I'll know more when we get her back to the infirmary."

"Murder! You're certain she didn't hit her head when she fell?" Markem was hoping that was the cause. The last thing he wanted was a homicide on board his ship.

"That's a pretty big drop, Doctor." The First Mate looked up to the deck where Yvonne's body had obviously come over the rail. "Isn't it possible the fall caused her death?" He fidgeted with his mustache.

The doctor removed her latex gloves and handed them to Nurse Brewer. "The most damage that fall could have caused, Wills, is perhaps some broken ribs or a fractured spine, but I don't believe it was the cause of her death."

"Please, Gwen, we need to be absolutely certain before I notify headquarters," Markem insisted.

"John, with all due respect, I investigated any number of murders as head of police forensics in Jersey. Believe me, she was murdered, probably on the deck above and tossed over the side. The killer probably expected her to go into the water and be lost at sea."

"Okay, Gwen, just get me a full report as quickly as you can." Markem knew he was projecting an apprehensive side of himself that his crew had never seen before, but this was his first shipboard murder and he didn't like it one darn bit. Not wanting to appear out of control, he composed himself by adjusting his tie and buttoning his jacket.

"The only question, other than who did it, is who exactly is she?" Nurse Brewer interjected.

"Awk. Bad lady. Man overboard."

None of them had noticed Taco perched on the rail a few feet away where he could hear what they were saying.

"This is no time for him to be here." Markem signaled a crewman to escort the bird elsewhere.

"Bad lady. Man overboard," Taco squawked again as he was being carried back to his perch in the infirmary.

"Sounds like…" the doctor exclaimed, "Taco may have witnessed whatever happened to her." She referred to the body in the lifeboat. "And if he's right, I believe the victim is one of the Silvers group. He's been hanging around them ever since we got under way."

"We should know soon enough," Wills told them. "Captain, I suggest we get the body to the infirmary as quickly as possible and keep this quiet until all passengers are back on board and we can ascertain exactly who she is."

*   *   *

At about the same time that Yvonne's sheet-covered body was discreetly being carried to the infirmary, Purser Boslow greeted a rather disheveled George Porter as he stepped aboard holding his passenger ID card.

"Welcome back, Mr. Porter. I'm sure your wife will be relieved to see you back on board again all safe and sound." He handed back the ID card.

"Yeah, it was pretty stupid of me, I guess." George tapped out his pipe into a nearby cigarette receptacle.

"It's happened before, sir. I assume our people in San Juan took good care of you."

"Oh, yes, I had a comfortable room and everything was fine, except for the lack of better scheduling on the part of the island-hopping flight service. I was a little concerned that I wouldn't make it back here on time."

"But you did, sir, and we're glad."

"Hello, George. Awk." Taco sat on the railing tilting his head as he greeted George.

"Hello, yourself." He returned the bird's greeting. "And now to face the music," George quietly said as he headed for his suite.

"Face the music. Awk."

CHAPTER 32

Suite 4B

Harriet Porter was in their suite reading. She looked up when George entered.

"Before you start, Harriet, allow me to explain." His clothes were rumpled and he appeared tired. "It's really the fault of the darn casino where I was playing Black jack. There are no clocks and they don't alert ship passengers about departures."

"Why are you so late getting back?" She frowned as she checked her watch. "It's after eleven."

"The darn island planes from San Juan aren't all that reliable. I found out that their posted schedules are nothing if not flexible, Harriet."

Her frown deepened. "I must say, George, your behavior has caused me embarrassment and undue aggravation. More importantly, how do you think it looks to Mel, and especially Yvonne Silvers, at a time when you might still be considered for that promotion?"

George knew she was more concerned about the promotion than his well-being.

"I know. I know. But it could have happened to anyone."

"Well, you should know that Yvonne commented on how careless you were to miss the boat. I'm sure that's going to affect her opinion of you."

"I'll apologize to everyone at dinner this evening. Right now I need a shower and some coffee."

"You look as though you didn't get much sleep either. I'll bet you played cards half the night."

"There wasn't much else to do, Harriet." He turned his back on her, stripped and tossed his clothes aside.

"I'm going on deck." She closed her book and tucked it into her bag. "You can meet me at the Lido Pool for coffee," she grumbled as he entered the bathroom.

CHAPTER 33

The Lido Pool

Wearing dark glasses, Harriet reclined on a lounge as she waited for her husband to join her. Suddenly she felt the lack of warmth as a shadow blocked the sun's rays. "George!" she exclaimed without looking up. "You're in my sun. Sit down, I've ordered coffee."

"I beg your pardon, Ma'am." Roger Wills stepped to one side as he addressed her. "You are one of the Silvers party, are you not?"

Harriet adjusted her top as she sat up. Tilting her glasses onto the top of her head, she responded, "I thought you were my husband, George. What did you ask me?"

"Are you with the Silvers group?" he repeated.

"Yes, unfortunately." Then she curbed her snippiness. "Yes, of course. I'm Mrs. George Porter. My husband is one of their key executives."

"There's been a mishap and I wonder if I can impose upon you to…"

As George approached Harriet, he saw Wills talking to her. "What's up?" he inquired.

"I take it you're Mr. Porter." Wills was relieved that George had appeared. Asking someone to identify a body was not a pleasant duty, especially if he had to ask a woman to do it.

"That's correct. I'm George Porter. If this is about my missing the ship the other day, I can explain exactly how…"

Wills' erect posture seemed to droop as he tugged on his tight collar. "That's not the problem, sir. As I started to say to Mrs. Porter, there's been a mishap." Wills felt foolish using that description for a murder. And since there was no easy way to put it, he addressed George in a soft tone as though that would make what he was about to say less horrible. "It's possible that we found the wife of one of your associates dead this morning."

"What? What did he say, George? Someone's dead?"

"Calm down, Harriet. I'm sure it's a mistake." He placed his hand on her shoulder to prevent her from rising. "What makes you think it's one of our group, Mr. Wills?"

Wills scanned the pool area thankful that there was no one else about except Taco squawking as he approached them.

"Hello, George. Awk." Taco paced back and forth a few times and then settled on the rail near them.

Ignoring the parrot, Wills replied, "Inasmuch as you and your wife are the only members of your group on board at the moment, it would help clarify things if you could identify the woman, Sir."

George gulped. "I've never done anything like that before."

Wills remained silent waiting for him to make up his mind.

Harriet had gotten up and was now standing beside them as they spoke. "Let's not get involved, George. Besides, everyone else has gone ashore. I had breakfast with them before they left, except for Her Highness, of course. Mel said he left her sleeping late as usual… oh my, George! You don't suppose it's…"

"Who might that be? Could it be the owner of this?" Wills reached into his jacket pocket and pulled out Yvonne's diamond necklace.

"I've never seen that before," George replied as he stared at the large stone.

"Of course you wouldn't know, George. It's Yvonne's. She was wearing it during dinner last night."

"If my wife is right, Mr. Wills, shouldn't you wait for Mr. Silvers?"

"The passengers who are still ashore aren't due back for a few hours yet. We'd like to be certain of her identity before unduly upsetting anyone else." Wills pocketed the necklace. "I'm sure you understand that."

"Yeah, I guess." George fiddled with his empty pipe, then turned to his wife. "Harriet, please stay here until I return. No point in both of us having to go through this ordeal."

"Oh George, how awful. Please hurry back."

"Hurry back, George." Taco flapped onto the arm of an empty deck chair and watched as George walked away with Wills.

CHAPTER 34

The Infirmary

Capt. Marchem waited anxiously as Dr. Gordon, assisted by Nurse Brewer, studied Yvonne's body on the examining table in the infirmary. A stainless steel, gooseneck floor lamp illuminated Yvonne's head as the doctor, wearing latex gloves, probed the area of the blow. "See the expanse of discoloration of the wound, Jamie, and the milky, bloody corneas." The nurse leaned in closer. "That's a sure sign she suffered massive brain damage. Considering the cold body temperature and the stage of rigor mortis, I'd say she died sometime after midnight. Hold on… what's this? Hand me those tweezers, Jamie." Pushing the light in closer, the doctor removed something from a corner of the wound. "Put this in a specimen bottle," she instructed.

As she held the tiny fragment up to the light, Nurse Brewer declared, "It looks like a tiny piece of foil paper with a shard of glass attached to it."

"Had to be on or part of the weapon," the doctor concluded. Turning to Markem who stood by listening to the gruesome details, she added, "There's very little point in going any further, Captain. I'm positive her crushed skull is the cause of death."

"She was definitely murdered then," the nurse confirmed.

"Without a doubt. Given the fact that she still had her necklace on, we can rule out robbery as the motive." Gwen Gordon now sounded more like a Jersey homicide cop than a cruise ship doctor. Her official persona had taken over. "Whoever did this probably knew her and was extremely angry." She pulled a sheet over Yvonne's dead body, snapped off the light, pulled off her gloves and tossed them into the trash. "Let's go into my office," she suggested. "We have to talk about this."

Seated at her desk, she addressed them both. "John," she called him by name again, "I know your concerns regarding the home office..."

"Yes, Gwen, it's bad enough the poor woman is dead, but murdered... that's not going to help alleviate our current shortfall of passengers. It will only add to the fears about cruising that have recently affected the entire industry." He ran his fingers nervously through his short gray hair.

"It's certainly not going to encourage cruising," Nurse Brewer added.

"That's true, but I'm afraid there's a bigger issue to consider..."

Just as the doctor was about to explain, there was a tap on the outer door. Wills entered along with George Porter.

"Excuse me," Wills apologized for the interruption. "I thought it imperative that we identify the woman as soon as possible. This is George Porter, one of the Silvers executives. He and his wife believe they might know who the victim is."

"I've never done anything like this before," George said so softly they hardly heard him.

"Aren't you the gentleman we left behind in San Juan?" Nurse Brewer smiled.

"'Fraid so. I just came back on board about a couple of hours ago. Sorry if I caused any inconvenience..."

"Not at all, sir." Markem rose to his feet, and grasped George's hand. The captain's authoritative demeanor seemed restored. "I'm sure this is difficult for you, Mr. Porter, but as you must realize, for obvious reasons, we need to confirm the identity of the poor woman as quickly as possible."

"I must admit that I'm quite apprehensive about all this, but I'll do the best I can."

"It will only take a moment and I'm sure you'll do fine," Dr. Gordon assured him. "Just follow me into the next room, please."

George complied as the others waited.

Standing rigidly beside the doctor, George watched as she removed the sheet covering just enough to expose Yvonne's face.

"Oh jeez! It is my boss, Mrs. Silvers." He stepped back quickly as if someone had pushed him. "What happened to her?"

The doctor replaced the sheet. "She suffered a fatal blow from a heavy object. That's all we know at the moment." She led George back out to the others.

"It's definitely Mrs. Silvers," the doctor announced. "Her full name, Mr. Porter?"

George was caught off guard by the question. "Huh? Oh, I'm sorry. This is quite a shock you know... it's Yvonne, Yvonne Silvers." He nervously pulled out his empty pipe then put it back in his pocket.

"Would you like a sip of water, Mr. Porter?" the nurse offered.

"Yes, please. Her husband is Mel, Mel Silvers. And her nephew Stuart is..."

George gulped the water.

"The nephew's last name?" Wills picked up a slip of paper and a ballpoint pen from the doctor's desk.

"It's Rosen, Stuart Rosen." After responding, George hesitated for a moment, then said, "If that's all, I have a very nervous wife waiting for me. I'm sure Harriet's anxious to know what's happened, especially since we know the dead woman."

"Do you have any idea who could have done this?" Dr. Gordon asked.

"No, but Yvonne made a habit of collecting enemies." He then went on to explain how cruelly she treated her employees up to and including her unexpected announcement a couple of nights earlier at dinner.

"That's very interesting," Dr. Gordon replied, then looked toward Markem.

"Mr. Porter," the captain addressed him, "let me explain the situation we have here. First, I will ask you not to divulge what you have seen…"

"But my wife…"

"Mrs. Porter is aware that we found a dead woman this morning," Wills interjected, "and she did identity Mrs. Silvers' necklace, Captain."

"I see. All right then, I suggest we have Mrs. Porter brought to my cabin where we can explain the circumstances we are dealing with. Is that satisfactory, Mr. Porter?"

"Sure, I guess so."

"Good enough, and as soon as we can, we'll notify Mr. Silvers and the nephew." Then Markem addressed the doctor. "Gwen, if we're no longer needed here, we'll be in my office."

"There is one thing I wish to discuss with you and Wills before you leave, Captain. Mr. Porter, would you please wait in the outer office. It's strictly a matter of company procedure. As a businessman, I'm sure you understand." It was apparent by his expression that he really didn't care one way or the other.

"Yes, of course," George agreed as he stepped into the outer office and closed the door behind him.

*   *   *

"Hello, George. Funny man." Taco swayed back and forth on his perch.

"Not now, bird." George pulled out his pipe, loaded it quickly and fired up, puffing anxiously as he waited.

"Smells good, George. Smells good."

"Yeah, I know, now eat your treats."

He stared at the closed door wondering what was going on in there and hoping he could leave soon.

*   *   *

Dr. Gordon spoke softly as Nurse Brewer, Wills and the captain gathered around her desk. "First, let me say that since this murder occurred last night while we were anchored off shore, it could very well mean that if we report this to the authorities in Aruba, the ship could be held in quarantine, so to speak, while the local police determine how to proceed."

Markem picked up on her meaning immediately. "That could be a real problem, Gwen. Not only the inconvenience and cost a prolonged delay would create, but we could possibly be subject to some kind of legal action if any of the passengers are subjected to awkward or unpleasant treatment."

"Sounds like a real mess," Wills added, "especially if we're dealing with international laws."

"I'm sure our own embassy would intervene on our behalf," Nurse Brewer offered.

"That would be just great," Markem exclaimed anxiously. "I'm sure the company would not appreciate any kind of government involvement, particularly a foreign government."

"Let me finish." The doctor regained their attention. "As I mentioned earlier, it's entirely possible that Mrs. Silvers was done in by someone close to her."

"I would say that seems logical," Wills agreed, "since robbery wasn't the motive."

"The severity of the blow would indicate to me," the doctor advised, "that it was delivered in keeping with the fury associated with a crime of passion."

"Well then, if it was someone close to her, say one of their group, that would rule out the remaining passengers," Markem sounded almost relieved.

"That could mean some sort of corporate intrigue," Nurse Brewer suggested, nodding her head in agreement.

With all of them of the same opinion, the doctor went on, "I would suggest, since Aruba was our last stop and it will take two days for our return to Fort Lauderdale, that we put Mrs. Silvers on ice and hold off reporting the problem until when we're back home."

"Can we do that?" Markem rubbed his chin. "What are the consequences, legally, I mean?"

"I see her point, Captain, and I think we can do it." Wills was leaning against a filing cabinet. "After all, we are an American registered ship and that would solve things as far as getting involved with any foreign red tape."

"We could put her in a food freezer," Nurse Brewer suggested.

"Is that sanitary?" Markem looked directly at the doctor.

"No problem," she quickly relieved his concern. "Everything is safe in a cold state. We can use the smaller dairy locker and transfer its contents in with meats. There's ample room since we have a short passenger list and we took on fewer supplies."

"Then do it," Markem instructed.

"Just one other thing," the doctor declared, "since we have the time, I suggest that Wills and I do a little probing among the Silvers group. Who knows, maybe we can nudge a guilty conscience into a confession."

"Fine, Gwen, but be discreet and don't jeopardize the company in any way." Markem reached for the doorknob. "Let's go, Wills, we've kept Mr. Porter waiting long enough. You gather Mrs. Porter and meet us in my quarters."

CHAPTER 35

The Captain's Quarters

Although the Coral Queen is the smallest ship in the Sea Venture fleet, Markem's quarters were well appointed. Adjoining his bedroom was a comfortable combination office and sitting room. The tan faux suede wallpaper and rich brown carpeting were in keeping with the masculine image of a ship's captain. Several photos of young Naval First Mate Markem in gold metal frames hung neatly spaced behind a small leather couch. Markem discreetly opened a window to dispel the faint smell of cigar smoke mingled with aerosol spray that had lingered in the room.

Markem greeted Harriet when she arrived, "Thank you for being so patient under such unpleasant circumstances, Mrs. Porter."

"I'm sure you'll be comfortable in this, Mrs. Porter." Wills directed her to a rich leather chair that matched the small couch George was occupying.

Still standing and looking directly down at her husband, she said, "What happened. Is it Yvonne, George?"

"She's dead, Harriet. Yvonne's been murdered," George blurted out in a quivering voice.

"That's awful, oh my." Stunned, she plopped down into the chair.

"Are you all right, Mrs. Porter? Can I get you something, some water, perhaps?"

"A bit of sherry, if it's not too much trouble, Captain."

As they watched Markem open a small cabinet, George was grateful she hadn't requested her usual martini.

"I'm afraid all I have is brandy, or I can call a steward…"

"Brandy will be fine. Oh, George, this is so distressing. Poor Yvonne," she sighed as she watched her brandy being poured.

"You may as well know, Harriet, I've already explained to the captain how much everyone detested her because of the way she treated all of her subordinates and about the animosity that prevailed after she announced that her nephew was being offered the promotion we all expected one of us would get." Turning to Markem he added, "Like I told you, Captain, she was a very difficult and abusive person, but to be brutally murdered like that, I just don't understand…"

"There's more than enough motive according to what you have explained, Mr. Porter." Wills had the ship's passenger list. "Now, just to double check, could you please give me the names of everyone in your group?"

"George, you don't really think any one of your associates could have done such a thing even as contemptible as she was, do you?" Harriet took a swallow of brandy.

Ignoring her, George proceeded to identify everyone in their group. "Of course, there's Harriet and myself…"

"Just a moment, gentlemen," she gulped, as she addressed Markem and Wills. "You're certainly not considering that we spouses are involved in this, nor my husband for that matter. He wasn't even on board last night, if you recall." She took another swallow of brandy.

George wanted desperately to get this over with, get her out of there and load up his pipe.

"Please, Mrs. Porter, at this stage no one's being accused of anything. And, of course, you're correct regarding your husband, which is all the more reason we require his assistance," Markem explained.

"Continue, Mr. Porter," Wills urged. "We still have the unpleasant task of informing Mr. Silvers and Mrs. Silvers' nephew."

As George rattled off the names, he watched Wills checking their cabin locations.

Once Wills had all the names, Markem thanked the Porters and then cautioned, "Until we notify Mr. Silvers and his nephew, I would strongly urge that you keep the matter to yourselves."

"Of course, Captain," George agreed but could only hope that Harriet would do likewise.

"Umph," Harriet gulped down the last drop. "Certainly," she stated as she dabbed her chin with her hanky.

As they were leaving, Dr. Gordon entered. "Everything has been properly taken care of, Captain. Hello, I'm Dr. Gordon," she addressed Harriet. "We dined together the first night out."

"Oh yes, I do recall. Nice to see you again." Harriet reached the door. "I need some air, George."

"Please keep us apprised of things," George said for lack of anything more appropriate to say.

"Yes, we will," Markem replied.

George opened the door for Harriet who stood waiting impatiently.

*   *   *

"Hello, George." Taco greeted them on the deck outside. "Awk. Hello, George."

"Does that fool bird have to be everywhere we go?"

"He's harmless, Harriet, probably just waiting for the doctor." Certain that she ignored him as she strode ahead, he loaded his pipe and followed.

When they neared B deck, she turned to him, "I must say, George, I'm not a darn bit sorry. She got what she deserved. I'm surprised someone didn't do it long before now."

"Talk like that can only make you a suspect, Harriet."

"Me and all the others who were on board last night. I wonder which one of them did it."

"I have a strong suspicion, from what little I heard earlier, that the doctor is going to pursue that very question."

"Well, I need a real drink and it's almost lunchtime."

*   *   *

"I have the list of the Silvers group, including the nephew who is quartered on C Deck," Wills informed the doctor.

"Good." She then turned to Markem. "I assume you'll be informing Mr. Silvers as soon as he returns."

"Of course. I must say I've had some difficult responsibilities as captain, but never one as difficult or as emotional as this."

"I know, John," she replied. "I understand how you feel and it might be best if I'm there with you when you tell him. Besides, first reactions are very important in a murder case. I'd like to see how he takes the news."

Wills nodded in agreement. "You might want to return her necklace to him as well, Captain." Wills handed over a white napkin in which he had wrapped the piece.

"Thanks, Roger." Markem placed it in his desk drawer. "Now, please instruct Boslow to be personally posted at the gangplank and explain to him that he should discreetly escort Mr. Silvers directly here as soon as he boards."

"Yes, sir. Do I tell Ken what's happened?"

"Let's keep this between us for the moment," the doctor suggested.

Markem concurred, then asked, "How do you plan to proceed, Gwen? I mean, are two days enough time to unearth a killer?"

"I'm not sure, John. It's not as though we have several detectives working on it. But I have seen suspects break down within hours under the right pressure of police interrogation."

"Ah, I needn't remind you that any false allegations could create lawsuit problems," Wills cautioned.

"We had some of those issues on the force as well, Roger. And you can rest assured, John, that we will do all we can to avoid any passenger problems. However, all we can really do is to lay out a strong scenario regarding what we suspect happened and then watch for an opening that would force a confession."

"Is that likely to happen?" Markem walked to a small fridge and pulled out a bottle of mineral water. "Gwen, Roger?" he offered mineral water to them also.

"Yes, I'd like some. Thanks, Captain," Wills replied as Markem handed him a bottle.

"No, John. Thank you. We still have a few hours before our day-trippers return and I need some time to pull my thoughts together. It's been awhile since I was one of the Jersey pros who did this for a living, so if you'll excuse me, I'll be in my cabin doing some planning. I'll return when you're ready to speak to Mr. Silvers." She picked up Taco, who had been waiting outside, and left them sipping their water.

CHAPTER 36

The Infirmary

Dr. Gordon deposited Taco on his perch in the outer office. When she entered the infirmary, Jamie Brewer was busy disinfecting the table they had examined Yvonne's body on.

Dr. Gordon took a chair facing her nurse. "Thanks for doing that," she said.

"You can take the nurse off the carrier, but you can't take the Navy out of the nurse," she quipped. "I cleaned so many operating units from tonsils to appendix, Gwen, that some nights I would almost forget to remove these." She snapped off the latex gloves she was wearing and tossed them into a stainless steel receptacle.

"I had days like that, Jamie; the only difference was my patients weren't going into a recovery room."

"Yeah, I guess not, and neither is Mrs. Silvers."

She watched as Jamie pulled a can of coke out of their mini-fridge, opened it, took a drink, then leaned back and relaxed. In spite of the current situation, Dr. Gordon considered herself fortunate in more than one respect. When she had made the choice to leave the force and apply for duty on a cruise ship, she had been a bit apprehensive. Even though she knew she was a good physician, the thought of being responsible for hundreds of live potential patients was a far cry from working in forensics. Having worked mostly in law enforcement where cordiality wasn't wasted on tough cases or suspects of all descriptions, she felt that the social interaction required of a senior crewmember would require some fine-tuning on her part. When she had been assigned to the Coral Queen, a deluxe, low-capacity ship, she had been very much relieved. That had been only half of her good fortune. Her nurse, Jamie Brewer, had not only proved to be a capable, efficient medical assistant, but a good friend as well.

"So, how do you plan to go about ferreting out the guilty party, Gwen?" Jamie's question suddenly interrupted Dr. Gordon's thoughts.

"It won't be easy. Although I've been part of enough police procedures to know how to go about it, the difference is we weren't dealing with self-indulgent business executives. We were dealing with criminals. Pushing the wrong buttons on these people could mean law suits and embarrassment to the company." Dr. Gordon realized that she had just stated the problem with the investigation she was about to undertake and shuddered at the thought.

"One thing's certain, Jamie; one of that group committed murder and John's hoping we can discover who before we reach homeport."

"Two days ain't much time, Gwen." Jamie shook her head, then took another swallow of her coke.

"I know."

CHAPTER 37

The Gangplank

It was shortly after the 6 p.m. first warning blast when Mel Silvers and his nephew, Stuart, climbed the angled walkway. They were chatting with a number of other returning passengers.

"I hope you've had a fun day on shore," Boslow greeted as they re-boarded.

"Viva Aruba," one of them responded in a slurred voice.

"Some more than others," Stuart joked.

"At least we walked off our lunch beers," Mel whispered to his nephew.

"More like sweated off. Boy do I need a shower. See you at dinner, Uncle Mel." Stuart headed for C deck.

Recognizing Mel from his boarding pass, Boslow addressed him quietly. "Would you be kind enough to accompany me to the Captain's office, Mr. Silvers?"

"Certainly, Mr. Boslow. Any idea what he wants with me?" Mel tucked his pass back into his wallet.

"I'm not sure, Mr. Silvers. I was instructed to escort you there upon your return."

"Don't tell me another one of my people is missing," Mel quipped as he followed the tall, well-pressed purser.

"Mr. Porter returned this morning, sir. That's all I know."

*   *   *

Boslow was dismissed as soon as he delivered Mel.

"Please, have a seat, Mr. Silvers," Markem invited. "I believe you know Dr. Gordon and First Mate Wills."

Mel remained standing. "Yes, of course. Good to see you again," he smiled in their direction. "Just what's this all about, Captain? I'm afraid I'm badly in need of a shower after my walking tour." Mel tugged on his sweaty polo shirt.

Dr. Gordon studied Mel closely as the captain continued.

"There's no easy way to put this, Mr. Silvers. I'm afraid your wife is dead."

"Did you say dead? Is this some kind of a…"

"In fact, she was murdered," the doctor blurted out. She did not intend to be cruel, but she wanted to read his reaction to her blunt statement.

Mel's knees buckled. Wills helped him into the chair he had been offered a moment earlier. "What do you mean? How?" His questions were followed by a pitiful moaning sound that was half sobbing and half wailing.

After allowing a moment for the shock to penetrate, the doctor answered, "She was found early this morning in a lifeboat." She held back the particulars.

Markem got out the brandy for a second time as Mel, still sobbing, struggled to compose himself.

"This might help." Markem offered him the drink.

"I don't understand." Mel spoke softly. "I left her asleep this morning…"

He accepted the glass and took a sip.

Wondering if her calculation as to the time of death could be so wrong, the doctor asked, "What time was that, Mr. Silvers?"

Sitting a bit more upright, he replied, "About 8:30. Rather than disturb her, I dressed quietly and left for my walking tour. Yvonne likes to sleep in, you know."

"Then you actually didn't see Mrs. Silvers this morning?" Markem inquired.

"No, not really. Her door was closed so I assumed she was still asleep.

Wills stood quietly nearby taking notes.

The doctor closely observed Mel's demeanor and sincerity, then went on to explain, "Obviously she wasn't in her room when you left, Mr. Silvers. She was discovered early this morning and I determined at the time that she had been dead for several hours."

"In a lifeboat?" He seemed to be more focused now. "How could she have...I'm sorry, did you say she was murdered?" Apparently that fact had just registered with him. "By whom? Have you caught them? Where is she now? I must see for myself. I mean, you could be mistaken, couldn't you? It could be someone else, couldn't it?"

"I wish we were mistaken, Mr. Silvers, but we got a positive ID from Mr. Porter shortly after he came back on board. And, of course, there's this." Markem retrieved Yvonne's necklace from his desk drawer and handed it to Mel. "I believe this belonged to your wife."

"Oh my." Mel grasped the jewel gently as though it were alive. "Yes, it's my wife's. She bought it recently. Last night was the first time she ever wore it." He sobbed as he held it. "Where is she now? May I see her?"

"Of course you may, but we should explain how we propose to deal with notifying the authorities." Markem went on to reveal their decision to wait until they were back in the States to avoid international red tape. "For this reason, her body is being kept in the dairy freezer. I do hope you understand and agree with our decision, Mr. Silvers."

"I guess that makes sense. Yvonne really hated the cold, you know," Mel sobbed. Rubbing his eyes, he assured them he was all right as he tucked Yvonne's necklace into his pocket. "I imagine her nephew, Stuart, should be told." Then he paused, "Oh my, Stuart may have been the last one to see her. They went off to have a private discussion after dinner. When I returned to our suite for the night, her door was closed, so I just assumed she was asleep."

Wills scribbled into his notebook, then said, "You should know, Mr. Silvers, no one, except for the Porters, is aware of this yet. We felt it best to await your return."

"I understand. I'll inform my nephew and the others as soon as possible."

"Dr. Gordon will escort you to see Mrs. Silvers now, and again, our deepest sympathy." Markem took the empty glass from Mel's trembling hand.

"Thank you, Captain." Mel then nodded to Wills, who was about to leave to assist Boslow who was checking in the other passengers returning from shore.

"If you'll please accompany me, Mr. Silvers," the doctor requested.

*   *   *

Alone in his office, Markem pondered this shipboard crisis. Certainly unexpected bad weather over the years had given him cause for concern over the safety of his ship and all aboard, but a murder! No amount of nautical skill and leadership training had prepared him for this. After serving as First Mate on a Navy destroyer in the South China Sea and then in the Tonkin Gulf pulling out heavily wounded men from Nam, Markem thought he had seen the last of violence. However, the one thing he had loved about the Navy was the opportunity to be at sea. Originally he was from a seacoast village in New England. Somewhere in his distant ancestry, there had to have been salt in his bloodline. After being discharged from the Navy, he had had the good fortune to apply to The Sea Venture Lines where he was given the rank of Second Mate on one of their larger Mediterranean cruise ships. Never having been married, the seafaring life suited him perfectly. Now here he was, after a few years of diligence and quite a bit of luck, the Captain of the Coral Queen. However, with all that experience, he still wasn't equipped to deal with a passenger being murdered aboard his ship.

Needing the calming effect of a good cigar, Markem left his cabin and located an isolated spot on deck. Firing up the Cuban, he stared out to sea. After a few relaxing puffs, he reflected on Gwen Gordon and the credentials she had presented when he had first reviewed her resume. At the time he hadn't been sure how an ex-police doctor would fare on a luxury cruise ship. However, over the past year, she had proven her worth as a comforting and compassionate shipboard physician. Now he was even more thankful for her presence. Her police background could be a definite asset in resolving this dilemma.

CHAPTER 38

The Dairy Freezer

Along the route to the dairy freezer, the doctor took particular note of Mel's behavior. As they passed a number of laughing, boisterous passengers, Mel, in his rumpled shirt and shorts, walked slightly bent over, obviously tuned out to their joyous activities.

"I'm sorry to put you through this, Mr. Silvers. It's not much farther."

"Thanks. I know it must be done, I just don't know how I'm going to cope with it all." He rubbed his already bloodshot eyes.

Gwen Gordon had seen enough homicide cases during her stint as a Jersey forensics cop to resist being swayed by what appeared to be spousal remorse. She knew that, according to statistics, seventy-five percent of murdered wives are killed by their husbands. From what she had heard, he probably had sufficient motive. Feigning compassion, she asked, "Exactly when did you see your wife last, Mr. Silvers?"

"I thought I mentioned that in the captain's office."

"No, actually, you said you assumed she was asleep when you returned to your suite last night and that you didn't want to disturb her."

"Yes, that's right."

"Then when did you see her last?" the doctor persisted.

"After dinner when she left the dining room with our nephew, Stuart."

They reached a bulkhead door marked 'Crew,' opened it and entered a service walkway leading to the food storage area. Unlike passenger corridors which were decorated with wood paneling and soft carpeting, the ship's service areas were finished in more functional materials: riveted steel walls painted off-white, rubberized flooring and brass handrails.

A short distance along the corridor, Dr. Gordon stopped in front of a door stenciled 'Dairy.' As she reached to open it, she turned to Mel, "I must caution you, Mr. Silvers, your wife died from a severe blow to her temple. The bruising and discoloration are quite extreme."

Mel nodded as he followed her in. It was a mechanical nod. He shuddered from the abrupt change in temperature inside and the anticipation of what lay ahead for him to see.

"We keep this room just above freezing," she explained.

Mel crossed his bare arms in an attempt to keep warm as they approached Yvonne's sheet-shrouded body. She had been laid out as respectfully as possible on a steel table.

"Oh no!" he cried out as the doctor uncovered Yvonne's head. "Who could have done such a horrible thing to her? Poor Yvonne, she enjoyed life so much." He slumped against a cabinet and started sobbing again, apparently forgetting the way she had treated him and their employees.

Dr. Gordon let the sheet slip back over Yvonne's face, took Mel by the elbow and guided him out into the warm walkway.

"My infirmary is fairly close, Mr. Silvers. Would you care to lie down? I can give you a mild sedative to help..."

"No. No, I don't believe in drugs, Doctor. I'll be fine. I'd prefer to return to my suite for a while. I've got to get out of these clothes and I need to shower."

"Very well. Allow me to show you the way. It's a bit confusing from here and, in your state of mind, I'd feel better about it if I accompanied you."

"Thanks. I suppose the best time to tell everyone is at dinner when they're all together," he remarked as he followed her. "I assume they'll be returning to the ship soon. I thought I heard the last warning blast, just before..." He choked up again.

"I believe you're right." She checked her watch. "The last warning goes off at seven and it's twenty after now."

When they reached Mel's suite, she suggested he rest if he could, then added, "If you don't mind, Mr. Silvers, I'd like to join you when you inform the others."

"That's no problem, Doctor." He unlocked his door and slowly entered. Before closing the door softly, he added, "I'll see you at dinner then."

*   *   *

Before returning to her office, Dr. Gordon took the stairwell leading to the upper deck. From there, she located the section of railing above the lifeboat the late Yvonne Silvers had fallen into. Imagining the time of the murder and knowing the degree of darkness that prevailed that cloud-covered evening, she concluded that the killer, not seeing the lifeboat directly below, assumed that he or she was dumping Yvonne's body into the silent sea. Given Taco's habit of perching anywhere along the ship's railings, and, if in fact he had witnessed the murder, he would have had a good view from that section of the deck. It would have been pointless to examine the immediate deck surface at that time. Any telltale signs of what had occurred there would have been removed by the early morning clean-up crews. They would have swabbed it thoroughly before Yvonne's body had even been discovered. Frustrated, Dr. Gordon ran her hands through her salt and pepper hair, loosened her collar button and, with nothing further to consider there, made her way back to her office. Until she could study the group's reaction to Yvonne's demise, there was nothing further she could do except hope for a miracle, something she knew seldom happened in the real police world.

CHAPTER 39

The Royal Palm Dining Room

It was 7:15 when Mel arrived for dinner. The Porters and the Dumonts were already seated.

Simon jumped up as Mel approached their table. Hugging him, he whispered softly, "We're so sorry for your loss, Mel."

"Thank you," he nodded. It was apparent to him that the Porters had spread the word already, even though they had been asked to keep it quiet.

"Here, sit next to me," Dina invited.

He automatically accepted.

"It's just horrible, Mel," Harriet exclaimed as she toyed with her martini glass.

"Jeez, Mel, Yvonne murdered, who could have…"

George's question was interrupted by the arrival of the Millers and the Dawsons.

"Hi, everyone," Jean greeted. "I hope you all enjoyed Aruba as much as we did."

"Why all the glum faces?" Barry asked as he pulled out his wife's chair.

"Yvonne's been murdered," Harriet blurted out.

"Please, Harriet, a little more sensitivity, if you don't mind," Mel protested.

"What in heaven's name is she talking about?" Helen Miller shook her head in confusion.

"Calm down all of you, and we'll explain," George insisted.

No one noticed Stuart arriving with the Collins.

"Good evening, everyone. I hope you don't mind my joining you again. It's no fun dining alone." Stuart slid out a chair for Marge Collin.

Before Harriet could blurt it out again, Mel spoke quietly but firmly. "There's no fun associated with this gathering, Stuart. You should know your Aunt Yvonne is dead."

"What are you saying, Mel?" Marge looked perplexed.

"Is this some sort of joke?" Bill Collin responded.

"If it is, it's not a bit funny, Uncle." Stuart was still standing.

"Just sit, Stuart, and I'll try to…" As he was about to explain, Dr. Gordon arrived.

"Good evening," she greeted. "Mr. Silvers and I thought it best that I join you. I assume they all know?" she addressed Mel.

"Know what?" Stuart snapped. "Just where is my aunt?" he insisted.

"Calm down, young man, and lower your voice," the doctor advised.

Mel was too drained to say anything further, so he let her take control.

*   *   *

"First of all," she cautioned them, "this is a very delicate situation and there's no need in upsetting or involving the rest of the passengers. Is that clear?"

"How dare you treat us in this manner," Stuart replied sharply.

"We're dealing with a murder on board and, to be perfectly blunt, it's obvious that one of you is the perpetrator."

"Are you implying that we had something to do with this?" Marge Collin unfolded and refolded her napkin.

"Think about it, Mrs. Miller, who else on board should we consider? We know it wasn't robbery since she was still wearing a very costly diamond necklace."

"Mel, is she saying that we're suspects?" Jean Dawson asked as she leaned against her husband.

"I'm afraid until we return to Fort Lauderdale, we're all under scrutiny," he admitted.

"I resent all of this," Harriet objected. "Why don't you speak up, George?"

"Calm down, Harriet. This is not the time for hysterics."

"Just how do you think my aunt feels at this point, Mrs. Porter?" Stuart countered.

This was just what the doctor expected, unguarded emotions.

"I understand your indignation; however, it's more than likely that Mrs. Silvers was murdered by one of this group and Capt. Markem has authorized me to conduct an investigation for the next two days during our return to Fort Lauderdale."

"This is preposterous," Dina proclaimed. "My husband is a sensitive artist. He could never…"

"I plan to question everyone, Mrs. Dumont, including you," the doctor stated flatly.

"What? You can't believe that Jean or I had anything to do with the poor woman's death!" It was the first time Jim Dawson had uttered an angry word since the cruise began.

Dr. Gordon didn't respond, instead she stood and addressed them all quietly so as not to draw the attention of other diners to what could become discord at the Silvers table. "This is not the place to continue this discussion. Please have your dinner. I will arrange for First Mate Wills and myself to speak to you individually starting in the morning. Good night." She was gone before they could object further.

*   *   *

"The last thing I want is to break bread with my aunt's killer," Stuart pushed his chair back in a huff.

"If I recall, young man," Marge told him, "You left with her after dinner last night…"

"Are you implying that I murdered her? You people are all sick, and your hatred for her was obvious to me in just the short time I spent with you."

"Stuart, calm down. In addition to losing Yvonne, this murder business has us all on edge," Mel admonished his nephew.

"I've nothing to hide." That was Stuart's last word on the subject as he walked away from the table.

After the reality of Yvonne's murder registered, the Silvers group nervously picked at their food. In the cold and suspicious atmosphere that ensued, the usual hearty appetites associated with cruising passengers all but disappeared.

CHAPTER 40

Suite 4B

George kicked off his Bally loafers, propped up his pillows and stretched out. "Did you notice, Harriet, there was not one sincere sign of remorse from any of them?"

"Does that surprise you, George? I mean, the woman was abominable. Humph, there's nothing to drink and they haven't refilled this," she complained as she opened the mini-bar.

He needed a drink himself. "I'll call room service." He leaned over and grabbed the phone.

"And that phony nephew," she continued, "he was very disrespectful toward her during dinner last night, and then they went off together to 'have a chat', as Yvonne put it."

"And just what did you do after dinner, Harriet?"

"Why? What do you mean? Oh, I certainly hated her enough but…"

"That's exactly what you're going to have to answer when Dr. Gordon questions you."

He could see how grateful she was when their drinks arrived and she accepted the tray from the steward. After handing George his gin and tonic, Harriet took a big slug of her martini. Appearing to relax a bit, she finally answered him. "I took a quiet stroll before retiring to our room."

"Alone?"

"What are you suggesting, George? Of course alone, except for that stupid parrot I saw wandering around the deck. Besides, I was upset and worried about your missing the boat."

He sat up. "Take it easy, Dear, but with no one to prove your whereabouts after dinner, I'm sure they're going to consider you a suspect."

"That's stupid and you know it, George. I'm a lot of things, but I couldn't harm a living thing. That includes that witch Yvonne."

"Stop referring to her that way, Harriet. Don't forget, like the rest of them, you're a suspect in her murder and every word you say will be scrutinized."

"I'm turning in." She sipped the last drop of her martini and disrobed. "If this foolishness persists, George, I want you to contact our attorney as soon as we reach Florida."

"Yes, Dear." Tired from the events of the day, he undressed, lowered the lights and slipped into bed while Harriet was still in the bathroom.

CHAPTER 41

Suite 5B

"This cruise has turned out to be a nightmare, Bill. First, you were told that the nephew was being offered the promotion you deserve, and now you're a murder suspect,"

Marge Collin complained as she adjusted her husband's trousers on the hanger he had just put in his closet.

"Please, Marge, stop fidgeting with every little thing. Where's the rest of that complimentary champagne?" he asked as he peered into the mini-fridge. "I could use a drink right now."

"I guess the maid tossed it. It was probably flat anyway." She folded his discarded t-shirt before placing it in the clothes hamper.

Bill pulled out a bottle of tomato juice, a poor substitute for champagne, and sat on the couch. "I'm far from the only suspect in this mess. If I understood the doctor's assertion, we're all included on the list of would-be-murderers."

"Be careful, Bill, tomato juice stains are hard to clean... what? What do you mean we all are? I'm not sad that Yvonne's gone, but why would anyone think I could be involved?" She flopped into the chair facing him and handed him a napkin.

"You wanted that promotion as much as I did, Marge." He set his drink down on a table beside the couch. "And where did you disappear to after dinner? It was past midnight when I came in and you weren't here."

She lifted the juice glass, wiped the ring it had made with a tissue and placed it back down. "If you must know, since you where so involved with your nightcap in the lounge, I took a little stroll on the deck."

"See what I mean, Marge? You were strolling when Yvonne got her head bashed in."

"Now, Bill, you know I couldn't have done such a terrible thing."

"I know, Marge, it would be too messy for you. But I'm not the one you have to convince."

"What about you, Bill? Did you stay with Barry and Helen in the lounge until you returned to our room?"

He drained the remainder of the juice and handed her the empty glass. "Not exactly. When Barry ordered a bottle of champagne, I had one glass. Then I left them and went looking for you."

"So you were out on deck alone also?"

"I wouldn't have been if you had joined us in the lounge."

"You know I don't enjoy drinking all that much, Bill, and I didn't want to put a damper on your evening. Besides, I'd had all I could take of Helen constantly telling me how much she missed her kids."

"I guess this means we're in for a lot of explaining tomorrow." He yawned and stretched."Are you coming to bed?"

"In a minute. I want to lay out some things for the morning."

He shook his head, turned over, and pulled up the covers while she fussed in the dresser drawer.

CHAPTER 42

Suite 6B

"The first thing I'm going to tell that doctor tomorrow is that she has one heck of a nerve to think for one minute that a Vietnam war hero would stoop to murder, even if the victim is someone as vile as Yvonne." Helen Miller was fuming when she and Barry returned to their room.

"Take it easy, Helen. She hasn't accused anyone yet." Barry wanted to light a cigarette but knew better in her presence.

"We shouldn't have ever come on this idiotic cruise. Besides, I miss the kids."

"You've called them every day, Helen, and they're fine."

"I hate what's happened, and for you to be a suspect in that nasty woman's murder… I just can't stand it."

"Any fruit left?" he interrupted as he scanned the room.

"No, it was getting soggy so I asked the maid to remove it." Looking in the mini-fridge, she added, "I guess she tossed the remainder of the champagne, too." She kicked off her shoes and rubbed one foot against the other.

"Oranges don't get soggy that quick, Helen."

"They felt soft to me."

Frustrated, he loosened his shirt collar. "You do realize that tomorrow we're in for a very aggravating day."

"What do you mean 'we'? How could you think I'm involved? You're the one who worked for that she-devil."

"I don't think for a minute you could have done it, Helen, but I'm sure you're going to have to explain your whereabouts after dinner."

More than a little offended by his insinuation, she asked, "What's wrong with you? I was in the lounge with you and the Collins."

"I know you were, but they're sure to tell the doctor you excused yourself before midnight. You'd better be prepared for some questions."

"I had to come back here and get out of my shoes. You know these new pumps were killing my feet... but I see what you're driving at, and it's preposterous."

"I know, Dear, so is this whole darn business." He pulled out a cigarette. "I need a smoke. I'll be on deck for a few minutes."

"That reminds me, Barry. When I returned to the lounge last night, the Collins told me you had gone on deck for a smoke."

"Like I said, we're in for an aggravating day tomorrow." He placed the unlit cigarette between his lips and opened the door. "Be back in five, Dear."

"I wish you would give up that terrible habit, Barry," she scolded as he closed the door behind him.

CHAPTER 43

Suite 7B

"I knew following Yvonne and her nephew after dinner last night wasn't wise, Jean."

"That doesn't prove a thing, Jim. I'm sure no one noticed me in that loud Fifties Lounge."

"I still don't see the point of it." He took off the white dinner jacket she had gotten for him at Nordstroms especially for this cruise. Just as she had planned, it was the perfect compliment to her black silk evening dress.

"Curiosity isn't a crime, you know," she added as she removed a black pearl hair clasp that also complimented her dress and her blonde tresses. "I just had to see the outcome of their little private talk. I wanted to be the first to know whether he accepted or not. If I've learned one thing in the business world, Jim, it's that early information can be invaluable."

"I hate this whole world you're in, Jean. It's full of deception, greed and insincerity. That's why I didn't join you on your silly lip-reading venture."

"You're such a wuss, Jim. You have to admit the rewards far outweigh a few minor negatives. Look at how well we're doing... and it's not from book sales." Jean paused, then asked him, "Just where did you go after I left you?"

"I came back here to read. That isn't a crime either."

"That figures," she scoffed. "Your nose is always stuck in a book, but that book can't verify your whereabouts."

"You know, Jean, I don't consider murder a minor negative. Now we're suspects and this isn't a mystery novel."

Ignoring the analogy, she opened the fruit basket cello-wrap. "Darn, the grapes are mushy."

"I guess we should have put them in the fridge to keep them cool."

"Yeah, I guess. Is that where the rest of the champagne is?" She reached down and pulled open the fridge. "Not here. Did you finish the bottle?"

"No, I thought you did."

"Oh well, forget it." She grabbed a bottle of club soda.

"You never did tell me what, if anything, you learned from your little exploit."

"If you must know, I couldn't make out a darn thing they were saying. All I know is that Yvonne left after only one drink and I slipped out a few minutes later."

"My goodness, Jean!" He raised his arms in dismay. "That practically puts you at the scene of the crime." He watched as she slithered out of her gown.

"You are joking, aren't you? I admit I hated her, but kill her, no thanks. That little chore was someone else's doing."

When she started removing her make-up, he brushed his teeth, put on his PJs and climbed into bed. He was always pleasantly distracted watching her nightly ritual, especially her fluid moves as she slipped into her teddy. He worshipped her but he couldn't help wondering deep down just how far she had become absorbed by the insatiable ambition he knew was driving her.

"Too bad the champagne's gone," she said as she turned out the light. "A little bubbly nightcap would have been good."

CHAPTER 44

Suite 8B

"Why in heaven's name didn't you speak up, Simon?" Dina Dumont complained.

Engrossed, Simon sat adjusting the focus of the Nikon aimed at her as she struggled to undo the clasp of her jade necklace.

"Please put that stupid camera away and help me with this." She kicked off a shoe in his direction as the shutter snapped.

Placing the 35mm gently on the table, he rose and, standing before her, unhooked the necklace with his arms around her. "You know you'll get wrinkle lines if you let stress get the best of you, Dina." He kissed her cheek, then handed her the strung jade.

"How can you worry about skin tone at a time like this? Don't you realize how serious it is to be suspected of murder?"

"Why do we have to worry?" He looked about the room. "Where's the rest of our champagne?"

"I have no idea. The way they tidy up these rooms twice a day, I'm surprised we can even see our footprints on the carpet."

"At least the fruit's still here." He unwrapped the cello carefully, then rejected a soft orange.

"Forget that, for heaven sakes." She hung her dress on a hanger and pulled on a robe. "Everyone knows how she always belittled and embarrassed you, Simon, and I truly hated her for that."

"She won't be doing that any longer, now will she?" He tossed a second orange into the wastebasket.

"That's just the point. They're all sure to tell Dr. Gordon how she treated you. You know it upset me enough to want to do her in on more than one occasion, and don't tell me your French temper didn't sometimes make you feel the same way."

"Don't talk like that, Dina, even in jest."

"Then you'd better be ready to explain why you left me alone for more than a half hour last night." She wanted him to realize the seriousness of the situation.

"Wait a minute. You know I was out on deck taking shots of the ship's lights reflecting on the water."

"You don't have to convince me, but I couldn't find you when I went out after you."

He picked up his camera. "The shots are in here to prove it, and isn't this a great turn of events. Now you tell me you were also out there alone."

"Nonsense, Simon. But so what? I know you don't have it in you to be lethal and I certainly don't either."

"Someone does, Dina."

"Yes, but it's not the Dumonts, and I'll be darned if they can prove otherwise."

"I hope it's as easy as that tomorrow." He tucked his Nikon into its protective case.

She opened her vanity bag and took out a bottle of Silvers Easy-Wipe nail polish remover.

As she saturated a cotton ball, Simon studied the remover bottle he had designed a few years earlier and recalled how critical Yvonne had been over its development. "One thing's for sure, Dina, it will be a lot easier in the office now."

"I'd keep that comment to myself if I were you, Simon," she advised as she capped the bottle and proceeded to the bathroom to rinse her hands.

CHAPTER 45

The Captain's Quarters

It was a bright, clear Caribbean morning as the Coral Queen made her way northwest on the return trip to Fort Lauderdale. The sun cast its warmth on the small sitting room table where Capt. Markem, Dr. Gordon and Wills were having a private breakfast meeting. Taco perched on the back of a chair near the doctor.

"I asked Mr. Porter to join us," Markem said as he smeared some marmalade on a crispy muffin.

"Makes sense," Dr. Gordon agreed. "His insights about each of his fellow associates can help us when we approach them regarding Mrs. Silvers' murder." She broke off a piece of muffin and offered it to the parrot. "Here you go, Taco, good boy."

Taco accepted it with his beak, placed it under a claw, and pecked off a chunk. "Here, Taco. Good boy."

"You're all right, Taco," Wills remarked. "Now if you could only tell us who clubbed Mrs. Silvers and tossed her over…"

"Man overboard. Bad lady."

"He said the same thing to Jamie and me when Mrs. Silvers' body was brought into the infirmary."

"Could be he's only repeating what he heard us discussing about how she might have been tossed over the side," the captain allowed.

"Over the side. Awk. Bad lady."

"We know, now eat your muffin, Taco," the doctor directed.

"Eat your muffin, Taco."

"Regular little chatterbox today, aren't you, Taco?" Markem chuckled as a knock on the door ended their interest in the amusing bird.

Opening the door, Wills welcomed George Porter.

"Come in, Mr. Porter. Join us. Would you like some coffee? A muffin?" Markem offered.

"No thanks, Captain, I just finished a very sumptuous breakfast." George took a seat at the table. "Hello, Taco," he greeted the parrot. "You seem to be everywhere."

"Hello, awk. Taco everywhere."

"Behave," Dr. Gordon said. "Thanks for agreeing to assist us, Mr. Porter. As you know, we must try to determine who in your group could have had enough animosity toward Mrs. Silvers to kill her."

"That's putting hate mildly," George replied.

This was precisely what Dr. Gordon expected to hear. "So I understand, Mr. Porter. Usually the husband is a party of great interest in a situation like this…"

George interrupted. "Excuse me, if you think Mel had anything to do with her death… look, I'm certainly willing to help with background on my associates and describe feelings they may have exhibited toward Mrs. Silvers, but in no way will I take part in accusing any of them of murder." He pulled out his empty pipe, nervously rolled it in his palm a few times, then pocketed it again.

"That's quite understandable, Mr. Porter," Markem replied. "However, I believe that the doctor was merely citing statistics."

"I'm aware of the 'husband is always a suspect' theory, Captain, having read a few police procedural mysteries."

Wills listened silently. His only purpose in being there was to take notes and, when called upon, to escort the suspects to and from the captain's cabin.

"Let me begin again, Mr. Porter," the doctor suggested. "Just give us any observations or perceptions you may have with regard to your co-workers' professional and personal relationships with Mrs. Silvers, including Mr. Silvers."

"That's simple enough, though I can't tell you much about her nephew. I only met him on one occasion before this cruise. According to my wife, however, he left alone with Yvonne right after dinner that night."

For the next half hour, Wills scribbled notes as George went through a further chronicle of his fellow executives and their relationships with Yvonne. With regard to their spouses, he further explained that his impressions of them were based solely on observing them at social functions.

"To be sure," he concluded, "you should understand that I disliked her as much as everyone else did. Yvonne wasn't a very lovable person. She ran the company with a tyrannical disregard for each and every one of us."

"You've been most helpful, Mr. Porter." Dr. Gordon stood indicating they were finished. "We'll no doubt be talking with you further. And please, explain to Mrs. Porter that our questioning of her is necessary but in no way accusatory."

Standing also, George shrugged his shoulders. "I tried doing that last evening and again this morning, but Harriet is the tense type and... I'm sure you'll handle her as best you can." Then he added,"As much as Harriet disliked Yvonne, it was more of a feminine discord. I know her too well, she couldn't hurt a fly."

Dr. Gordon nodded amiably, having heard the fly bit before.

"I can assure you, we'll be most tactful with everyone," Markem said, "especially Mrs. Porter, considering her anxiety over the matter."

George thanked them, then automatically pulled out his aromatic tobacco and pipe. He was ready to load as soon as he departed.

"Smell good. Awk."

"You're quite a character, aren't you, Taco?" George said as he passed the bird.

"Quite a character," Taco repeated. "Funny man."

As soon as Porter closed the door behind him, Gwen addressed the captain and Wills. "Usually the husband is the numero uno suspect. However, in this situation, since the nephew was obviously the last person to see the victim alive, let's start with him." Then she added, "In fact, let's save Mr. Silvers till later. Porter didn't have too much to say about his boss. Perhaps our discussions with the others will be more revealing."

"Sounds like detective work is mostly conjecture," the captain observed as Wills left to locate Stuart Rosen.

"Crime solving is often a lot of luck mixed with coincidence," the doctor replied. "But in this case, we at least know the murderer is still among us and is probably as nervous as a cornered mouse."

"Cornered mouse," Taco echoed.

"Maybe our little friend here should get some fresh air," Markem suggested.

"Fresh air. Get some fresh air."

As Dr. Gordon invited the bird onto her forearm, Markem expressed one more concern. "Do everything you can, Gwen, to solve this. Otherwise, when we reach Fort Lauderdale, I'm certain the authorities will quarantine the ship. With the local police taking over, it will create one very huge problem, not only for all the other passengers, but for the company as well."

"I'll do my best, John. Like I said, with a little luck, we can crack this."

She carried Taco out onto the deck. In spite of the beautiful balmy morning, Gwen couldn't help getting that familiar feeling of pressure most cops get at the beginning of an investigation. All she could think of at the moment was how she would much rather be enjoying the pleasant life of a cruise ship doctor instead of interrogating a bunch of egotistical people, one of whom was a murderer.

Nurse Brewer appeared interrupting her thoughts.

"Gwen, I'm glad I caught you alone. I thought you should know that I took a close look at that shard of glass and speck of paper we found on Mrs. Silvers."

"Oh?"

"Yeah, and I'm pretty sure it's bottle glass, so I went into the dairy freezer and studied the blow on her head…"

"And?"

"The bruise looks like a dent that could have been made with a bottle. That could explain the glass shard and piece of paper which looks like it might have been part of a label."

"That could very well be, Jamie, and darn it, I couldn't see anything on the floor of the upper deck when I finally checked it out."

"I'm sure it was swabbed as usual early the following morning."

"Well for the moment, Jamie, let's just keep this between the two of us."

"There's one more thing, Gwen, and this is a real wild guess. That piece of label had a trace of green ink and, if I'm not mistaken, it looks like it could have come from the complimentary Chateâu Émeraude champagne placed in every cabin."

"Goodness, Jamie, are you sure you were an Army nurse and not a cop? If you're right, that identifies the heavy blunt object. A champagne bottle is certainly a perfect club."

"Perfect club, man overboard. Awk," Taco chattered as Dr. Gordon held her arm close enough for him to perch on the deck rail.

"I'd be willing to bet he saw the murder," Jamie declared.

"It's quite likely, especially since he wanders all over this ship night and day."

Spotting Wills approaching with Stuart, the doctor again cautioned, "Not a word of this to anyone."

"Gotcha. I'll be in the infirmary if you need me."

"Okay, and take our possible witness with you."

"Some witness." Jamie coaxed the bird onto her arm.

CHAPTER 46

The First Suspect

"Mr. Rosen, thanks for coming so promptly." Dr. Gordon greeted Stuart as Wills escorted him into Capt. Markem's cabin.

"Yeah, sure. You told us all last night that we'd be questioned regarding my departed aunt, so let's get on with it," Stuart replied sullenly.

Here we go with the first nasty. "If you'll join me in the captain's office, we'll make this as brief as possible," you little twit.

"Thanks for coming, Mr. Rosen," Markem said.

Wills remained near the door notepad in hand.

"I'm here, so what is it you want to know?"

"Why don't you have a seat," the doctor suggested.

Markem slid out a chair for him.

Stuart gripped the back of the chair. "I can't imagine this will take that long." He remained standing. "After all, I am grieving over my aunt."

"As long as it takes for you, Mr. Rosen, to explain your activities from after dinner last night until one in the morning."

"That's easy, I was aboard this ship."

The best way she knew to deal with his surliness was to get directly to it. "That's not quite good enough, sir."

"I suggest you take a seat, Mr. Rosen." This time Markem sounded more insistent.

"This is crazy." Stuart sat. "I'm not sure you people even have the right to conduct this sort of investigation..."

"You're absolutely correct, Mr. Rosen," the doctor cut him off. "If this were, as you say, an investigation. But it's not," she lied. "It's merely an inquiry at this point with no legal significance except for the rules of the sea, in which case the Captain has jurisdiction. Unless, of course, you'd care to confess..."

"Confess! To what?" he snapped. "Okay, so I hated my aunt. That's no crime. They all did."

"Be calm, Mr. Rosen," Markem advised. "Just tell us your activities from the time you and Mrs. Silvers left the dining room together last night."

"This is stupid." Stuart paused shaking his head. "Okay, I'll play along with your rules of the sea game, but only because I have nothing to hide."

"Good, so please proceed," the doctor urged. She was hoping he was the killer. She disliked him that much.

"I suppose Uncle Mel already told you that my aunt offered me a job, which I flatly turned down. It was a bogus offer because she knew I was planning legal action against her and the company for personal reasons. She was just wicked enough to think that I would accept the job and call off my suit against Silvers, even at the cost of bypassing one of those poor saps who was certainly more capable and more deserving of the position. She was a horrid person, but I didn't kill her."

"How did she react to your declining her offer?"

"We were in your Fifties Lounge having a drink when I turned her down." He paused. "I think I'd like a cup of coffee, Captain." He pointed to the carafe across the table.

"Of course. Wills, would you mind?" Markem requested.

Remaining silent, Wills obliged and then returned to his post near the entrance.

"And?" Dr. Gordon persisted. "Then what?"

Stirring his coffee slowly, obviously to annoy her, he finally took a sip and continued. "She was extremely angry with me. I'm sure it was not so much that I refused but she realized her scheme to get me to call off the legal action I had planned hadn't worked. She finished her brandy and stormed out."

"And then what did you do?"

"As she was leaving, I told her that I was going to enjoy my bottle of champagne at her expense and stay there and reminisce over the fifties."

"Did anyone see her leave without you?"

"You know it's funny, there was that young lady, I believe she's their merchandising person, off in a corner. She was alone having a drink. I don't know if she saw us or not."

"Did that young lady leave first, or did you?"

"I really can't say, Doctor. More people came in and obstructed my view of her table. Besides, I was into my bubbly and enjoying the fact that I had really ticked off my aunt."

"You realize, Mr. Rosen, you were most likely the last person to see your aunt alive and only a short distance from where she was murdered."

"Yeah, I guess."

"When did you leave the lounge?"

"Like I said, a bunch of people came in. It's really a small room, Captain," he commented.

"It's a small ship, Mr. Rosen," Markem replied.

"What time did you leave?" Dr. Gordon kept at him.

"I didn't notice the time. Like I said, it got crowded, so I finished my drink, grabbed the bottle and left. Must have been shortly after my aunt departed."

Jeez, she thought, this guy's incriminating himself. It can't be this easy. "Did you see your aunt again outside?"

"No, I headed straight for my cabin." He finished his coffee and set the cup down hard on the saucer underscoring his impatience.

"One last question for now, Mr. Rosen. Did anyone see you from the time you left the lounge until you reached your cabin on…" she looked toward Wills.

"C deck," Wills replied.

"No, no one. No one I knew, that is." He rose from his chair. "Except that darn parrot, and someone further up the deck."

"Then you did see somebody after leaving the lounge? Did you recognize them?"

"No, it was just some guy. It was rather dark, but I think he had a beard."

"Did he see you, this man with a beard?" she asked skeptically.

"It's hard to say. It was overcast, and like I said, dark. Now, is that all?"

"Yes, for now. And thanks, Mr. Rosen." Dr. Gordon nodded. "And please, let's keep this little discussion to ourselves."

"Yeah, right."

Wills stepped aside after opening the door for him. "Thanks for your cooperation," he said quietly as Stuart exited shaking his head.

"What do you think, Gwen?" Markem asked once the three of them were alone.

"He could have done it," Wills volunteered before she could respond. "He's certainly arrogant enough and he did hate his aunt."

"That's true," she agreed, "and Jamie and I are now almost positive the murder weapon was one of the ship's champagne bottles."

"A champagne bottle, Gwen?" Markem appeared confused.

"How did you determine that?" Wills questioned.

"The shard of glass and fragment of foil label we found in the concave indentation in Mrs. Silvers' skull appears to indicate as much. The bottle obviously cracked from the impact," Dr. Gordon explained.

"How about that?" Wills checked his notes. "Rosen said he left the lounge with a bottle."

"And he was at the crime scene," the captain added.

"Exactly," she replied.

"Then shouldn't we detain him or cross-examine him further?" Markem asked insistently.

"On the surface he appears to be our man, but consider this, would either of you openly admit to having carried the murder weapon out of the lounge?" Gwen could see the disappointment on their faces as they considered her rationale. "Besides, everyone of them had access to a champagne bottle, compliments of the Coral Queen."

"I still think we should pressure him a little more," Markem declared.

"There's one thing you both best understand," she clarified, "unless we have an eyewitness or we can induce a confession from someone, there's very little we can do except question them all until we reach port and the authorities take over."

"I'm hoping we can avoid that, Gwen," Markem grimaced.

"I know, John."

"What about the bearded guy?" Wills asked.

"Yes, what about him?" Markem sparked at the thought ready to follow any lead no matter how slim.

"John, it could have been a member of the crew. If I'm not mistaken, a couple of them have beards."

"We can at least have Mr. Rosen take a look at them. Maybe his memory will be triggered," Wills said.

"Okay, but I believe we should start by checking the crewmen with beards to see if one of them saw Mr. Rosen on deck that night. If not, we can see if he recognizes one of them," she offered.

"Makes sense," Markem concurred. "So who's next?"

"Let's stay with continuity and talk to Ms. Dawson. We know she was in the lounge at the same time as Rosen and close to the scene of the crime as well."

"I'll bring her right in," Wills told them. "Then I'll locate our bearded crewmen and check them out."

"That's great, Roger." Dr. Gordon poured herself some orange juice and plopped into a nearby chair. "Now you know why I gave up the Jersey Police Department for a cushy job at sea."

"I thought being captain was cushy until this darn murder." Markem poured himself some more coffee while they waited for Jean Dawson.

CHAPTER 47

The Second Suspect

Wills located the Dawsons having a late breakfast with the Millers on the Promenade Deck. They were shielded from the brilliance of the morning by a large green and pink striped umbrella.

Approaching their table, Wills politely addressed Jean Dawson, who was further shaded by a wide-brimmed straw hat. "Sorry to interrupt, Mrs. Dawson, but when you're ready, the Captain and Dr. Gordon wish to speak with you in the captain's cabin. But please don't rush your meal, I'll be happy to wait."

"Why me first?" Jean asked snappishly looking up at him from under the brim of her hat.

"I'm not privy to the order they've chosen," he lied.

"Shouldn't I be with my wife?" Jim Dawson volunteered.

"I was specifically told one person at a time, sir."

"Don't worry, Jim, they'll get around to spouses after the rest of us drones," Barry Miller assured him.

"This is all too horrible," Helen Miller moaned. "I wish I had never come on this fool trip. I miss the kids, Barry."

"I know, Dear, but we can't get to Florida any faster, so we should try to make the best of it."

Ignoring all the side play, Wills offered, "Shall I come back for you in a few minutes, Mrs. Dawson?"

155

"No. I'm finished. Let's get this over with." She stood and tossed her napkin into her empty chair.

"I'll be waiting for you by the Lido Pool, Jean." Her husband gave her elbow a reassuring squeeze.

"And when you're ready for me, Mr. Wills, I'll be with Mr. Dawson," Barry declared.

"I appreciate that, Mr. Miller. If you'll follow me please, Mrs. Dawson," Wills invited cordially.

*   *   *

After an amicable greeting, Dr. Gordon got right to it. "This shouldn't inconvenience you too much, Mrs. Dawson, as long you can explain why you were alone in the Fifties Lounge the night Mrs. Silvers was murdered." The doctor had positioned herself directly across the table from Jean, and Wills was once again stationed at the door.

"How did you know?" She removed her hat and placed it on the chair next to her.

"Oh, I see, you've spoken to her nephew."

"Please just answer the question, Mrs. Dawson," the doctor insisted.

"There's no harm in having a drink in that Lounge. After all, I'm a guest on your ship, Captain." She addressed her comment directly to Markem who was sitting quietly next to the doctor.

"Of course not, Mrs. Dawson. However, if you'll just answer Dr. Gordon's question, you will understand the relevance of your presence there."

"Well, if you must know," she stared directly at the doctor, "since we were told earlier by Yvonne that her nephew was being offered the job one of us expected to get, I took it upon myself to follow them to observe his reaction to her proposal."

"I see. And what did you learn from this scouting expedition?" the doctor inquired facetiously.

"There's no call to make light of my actions. I was just curious and it was important to me," Jean replied caustically.

"We're not interested in the professional intrigue behind your being there, Mrs. Dawson. Our real concern is that it places you practically at the murder site." Dr. Gordon studied Jean as she told her this, but could read little from her attractive face.

"Hold on, Doctor," Jean rebutted, "I stayed there until I saw Yvonne's nephew leave. If anyone is suspect, wouldn't he be?"

Ignoring the suggestion, Dr. Gordon continued, "Can anyone verify when you left and where Mr. Dawson was at the time?"

"Jim was in our suite reading. As for the young girl who waited on me, I'm not sure she would remember. She got busy with a group of people who came in at about the same time. I signed my check and left shortly after I saw Stuart Rosen leave, just like I said."

"And you didn't see anything unusual on that part of the deck when you left?"

"No. The light was dim and it was quiet until, from out of nowhere that stupid parrot squawked and scared me half to death."

"Did you happen to see a bearded man in the area?" Markem asked.

"No, I didn't see anyone." She looked from the captain to the doctor and back again. "Is there anything else?"

"Not for now. Thank you for cooperating, Mrs. Dawson." So far all Dr. Gordon had managed to ascertain was that Stuart Rosen's and Jean's stories fitted together.

"Thank you, Mrs. Dawson, you've been most helpful." Markem smiled, walked around and held her chair.

Wills tucked his notebook in his pocket and quickly opened the door for Jean. "Thank you again, Mrs. Dawson," he said with a smile.

Gwen Gordon couldn't help observing that even Wills was not immune to Jean Dawson's attractiveness.

CHAPTER 48

The Third Suspect

"Thanks for obliging us, Mr. Dawson," Dr. Gordon greeted Jim Dawson when he and Wills arrived.

"Yes, thanks, Mr. Dawson," the captain echoed. "Please have a seat." Markem pointed to the chair across from the doctor. "Coffee?"

"Thanks, no." Dawson sat where the captain indicated. "I'm not sure how I can contribute to your inquiry," he stated as he removed his sunglasses and continued babbling. "There is no way my wife could harm anyone, even someone as awful as that woman. I must confess that I hated for her to work there…"

Dr. Gordon, Markem and Wills listened as Dawson carried on. From the doctor's experience, he was the ideal person to interview. He needed no coaxing.

"I mean, you just spoke to Jean. You must have seen how amiable she is. And completely devoted to her work at Silvers in spite of how I feel about the place… Oh boy, listen to me… I'm sorry." He quit like a dead battery.

"It's perfectly normal to defend your wife, Mr. Dawson, and please understand we haven't accused her of anything. Our brief chat with her was to gain insights into her relationship with Mrs. Silvers."

"We also inquired how the others felt about Mrs. Silvers," Markem added.

"Uh... I merely thought you should know how gentle a person Jean really is..."

"Relax, Mr. Dawson," Markem suggested. "Mrs. Dawson comported herself extremely well. With regard to yourself, we would like to know your whereabouts after dinner last night."

"We already know that your wife left you to eavesdrop on Mrs. Silvers and her nephew," Dr. Gordon took over.

"I think eavesdropping is a rather crass way of explaining her curiosity over a potential promotion. Wouldn't you say?"

It's obvious all men find Jean Dawson ingratiating, Dr. Gordon thought. "Okay then, Mr. Dawson, let's just agree that her presence was verified by Mr. Rosen who spotted her in the Fifties Lounge while he was meeting with his aunt."

"Jean told me that she had already admitted that," he confirmed. "It was a harmless attempt to learn if he was taking the job she wanted so very much. She couldn't make out what they were discussing, so she left."

"And the moment she chose to leave, by her own admission, was right after Mrs. Silvers did," Dr. Gordon pressed the point.

"So-o-o?"

"So-o-o, it places your wife at the murder scene." Dr. Gordon studied his face as she drove the fact home.

"Oh my." He fiddled with his glasses.

"Now the only way to help," Dr. Gordon paused for affect, "is to explain where you were during that time and exactly when you saw your wife again."

"After dinner we all went our separate ways. There was no point in lingering over drinks and small talk, especially following Yvonne's announcement that she was offering her nephew the Senior Vice-President's job."

Talky aren't you? the doctor thought. But then with a dynamic wife like yours, who can blame you for spouting off when you have the chance. "And which separate way did you go, Mr. Dawson?"

"When Jean and I parted, I took a brief stroll about the upper deck."

"Did anyone see you?"

"If they did, I have no knowledge of it. Besides, as I said, it was a brief stroll. From there I went directly to our cabin to read. I'm halfway through the life story of 'The Genius of Nikcola Tesla.' It's fascinating, if you've never read about him, Doctor."

"I'm sure it is, Mr. Dawson." Give me a break. "Just what time was that?"

"After my stroll, I'd say, oh, I was back in our cabin by 11:45 or thereabouts."

In addition to her own impatience, Dr. Gordon could see Markem fidgeting to have Dawson get on with it. "And Mrs. Dawson?" The doctor felt as if she were extracting a wisdom tooth.

"What about her?" he asked.

"What time did she return to your cabin, Mr. Dawson?" Wills finally broke his silence.

"About 1:00 or 1:10. I remember commenting that our travel alarm was a bit slow."

No more than you are. "Did Mrs. Dawson appear upset when she returned?" The doctor almost hesitated to ask for fear of getting another roundabout reply.

"Of course she was. After having gained nothing from her observations in the Fifties Lounge… oh, I see, you mean, did she seem distraught for another reason?"

"Yes. Did she act strange or frightened?"

"No, just ticked off that she had wasted her time there."

Having gotten all she could from Jim Dawson, Dr. Gordon turned toward Markem. "I believe Mr. Dawson has explained everything for now, Captain, unless you have something further you wish to ask him."

Markem shook his head, then said, "Thank you, Mr. Dawson. If need be, we'll speak with you again."

Wills opened the door and waited, but Dawson remained seated. "I'm fully prepared, Captain, to answer anything further, but I must insist that you have no basis for suspecting my wife or me for the foul murder of Mrs. Silvers in spite of how much we disliked the woman."

"You've made that abundantly clear, Mr. Dawson." The doctor rose and went to the door. This time Dawson did likewise, put on his sunglasses, and bid them good-day.

Markem got up and stretched. "My goodness, he's very precise, isn't he?" he commented as soon as the door was closed behind Dawson.

"Too much so to bludgeon anyone," Wills declared.

"True," Dr. Gordon agreed.

"So what do you conclude so far, Gwen?" Markem asked.

"I'm not sure we've interviewed the killer yet, but we'll see. Who's next?"

Before Wills could respond, Markem announced, "I still have a ship to run. Let's take a half-hour break and then speak to…" He looked toward Wills.

"I would say Mr. Collin, if you agree, Gwen." Wills checked a list. "He's their VP of Sales."

"It's Mr. Collin in half an hour," she concurred. "See you both back here then."

CHAPTER 49

The Fourth Suspect

When Wills located Bill Collin, he and Marge were sunning at the edge of the Lido Pool with the Dumonts and Mel. The Dawsons, Porters and Millers were chatting under a nearby canopy.

"Excuse me, folks," he interrupted, then addressed Bill Collin directly, "if you wouldn't mind, Mr. Collin, Capt. Markem and Dr. Gordon would like to speak to you now."

Removing his sunglasses, he squinted up at Wills. "Sure. Why not?" He sat up and searched under his lounge for his sandals.

Pointing at Taco perched on the back of an empty lounge, Wills asked, "Is he behaving?"

"A bird on a cruise ship, humph," Harriet mumbled into her martini glass.

"I must say that he's an awfully chatty bird," Marge Collin protested. "Here, Bill," she handed her husband his sandals.

"Chatty bird. Awk."

"If he's a bother, I'll take him back to…"

"The bird's no problem." Simon aimed his Nikon at Taco. "Besides, he's a real ham for the camera."

"Real ham," echoed Taco.

"I think he's rather pleasant to have around," Jim Dawson added, looking up over the edge of his book.

"If you say so, Sir."

"How is it going so far?" Mel inquired nervously.

Assuming the Dawsons had told the others how things were being conducted during their interviews, Wills replied, "We're merely trying to gather any information that will be helpful regarding this terrible tragedy, Mr. Silvers. I'm sure Capt. Markem will get back to you as soon as possible."

"Yes, of course he will. Thanks."

As he was about to leave with Wills, Marge grabbed hold of her husband's arm. "Just a minute, Bill, your shirt collar's turned in." She adjusted it. "There, that's better, dear."

"That's better, Dear," Taco repeated.

Jean Dawson and Dina Dumont smiled knowingly at each other.

"Stupid bird," Marge muttered as she automatically smoothed her shorts before sitting back down.

"Lead the way, Mr. Wills," Collin gestured.

"Mrs. Collin seems like a very attentive person," Wills commented after he and Collin left the group.

"Marge is that and more. Are you married, Mr. Wills?"

"No sir, but I hope to be fortunate enough to find the right person someday."

"Choose wisely, Mr. Wills, choose wisely."

Wills detected a slight trace of melancholy in the advice. "I will, Sir. Ah, here we are, Mr. Collin." He knocked, then opened the door and held it for him.

*   *   *

After Dr. Gordon had reassured him about their motive for questioning all of them, Bill Collin took a seat across from her without being instructed to do so. She sensed that he was confident and cool about his presence there. For the benefit of Markem and Wills, she commented, "You seem quite at ease, Mr. Collin. I assume the Dawsons explained that we're merely checking on everyone's whereabouts the night in question."

"No problem," he said with a smirk. "Heck, when you're in sales you come up against a lot of pressure, especially with buyers. So compared to that, Doctor, this is a walk in the meadow." His grin turned to a slight chuckle. "I'm not so sure the wives are going to be as patient about any of this, though."

"I'm glad you understand, Mr. Collin, and I hope your associates do as well. Would you care for coffee?" Markem offered.

"No thanks, Captain."

"I'm happy you're so at ease, Mr. Collin. So let's get right to it," Dr. Gordon prodded. He's a smooth one. "Exactly where were you between midnight and 1:00 a.m. that night?"

"Right to the point huh, Doctor? Okay, immediately after dinner Marge, the Millers and I slipped into that little bar area just off the dining room for a drink. When Barry lit a cigarette, Marge complained. He ignored her, so she got up and left. My wife's not much of a drinker anyway."

"Do you know where Mrs. Collin went after she left you?"

"She told me later that she took a walk on deck and then went back to our cabin."

"And what time was that?"

"I don't know. I'm guessing maybe around 11:30 or 12:00." Then he looked directly at Markem. "There's no clock in that bar, you know."

"It's meant to be a relaxing atmosphere, Mr. Collin. Cruise activities aren't meant to be measured by time."

"That's some spiel, Captain, you should be in sales," Collin quipped.

"I'm afraid it's right out of our corporate manual," Markem joked back.

Annoyed by the side play, Dr. Gordon cut in, "So I suppose, Mr. Collin, lacking a clock in the bar, you can't tell us what time you left."

"Oh, sure I can, Doctor. After a few sips of champagne that Barry had ordered, I took off looking for Marge. That was about twenty minutes after she left." He then grinned as he pointed to the gold Rolex on his wrist.

Very cute. "And where did you look for her?"

"I roamed around deck for a few minutes, then headed for our cabin."

"Were you with anyone or did you see anyone during your roaming?"

"No, in fact..."

At that moment there was a knock on the door. It was Purser Ken Boslow. He whispered something to Wills.

"I'm sorry to interrupt, Captain," Boslow apologized as he and Wills approached Markem.

Assuming it was some navigational or other problem with the ship, Markem aimed an open palm at Dr. Gordon. "Just hold on for a minute please, Doctor, Mr. Collin."

Collin smiled and leaned back. "Sure, no problem."

Dr. Gordon's attention focused on what had caused the interference.

"Captain, I thought you should know that we have another missing passenger," Boslow spoke in a low tone. "I was going to wait to inform you until you were finished here, but given the current situation, it seemed best to tell you right away."

"Oh, for heaven's sake, not again," Markem exclaimed.

"Sorry, Gwen," Boslow apologized.

"No harm, Ken, you did the right thing," she assured him.

"Yes, of course, Ken," Markem agreed. "Now, who is it this time and what happened?"

"It's a gentleman who boarded in San Juan, sir. His name is..." Boslow referred to a small logbook, "Marshall, Herb Marshall. He got off in Aruba and never returned."

Collin startled them when he burst out loudly. "What! What was that name?"

"It's Marshall, Herb Marshall. Is there something wrong, Mr. Collin?" Wills was the first to react to the interruption.

"This is either some sick joke or the weirdest coinci-dence I've ever encountered," Collin replied.

"Excuse me, Mr. Collin, but a missing passenger is hardly a joke and two on the same cruise is unheard of. Now please, do you know this gentleman?" Markem's tone was urgent and authoritative.

"It's just that Herb Marshall is the name of the man who used to be our boss at Silvers."

"Used to be?" Dr. Gordon picked up on his point.

"Doctor, perhaps we should take a short break," Markem suggested. "I'd like to deal with this matter in private."

Seeing that he was distracted with this additional problem, she agreed. "Of course, Captain, and if it's all right with you, Mr. Collin and I can remain here until you return." Her instincts told her to continue questioning him.

"Of course, Gwen. Thanks for understanding, Mr. Collin." Markem got up and headed for the door. "Be back shortly. Ken, Roger, let's sort this out. We do have information regarding this Marshall, don't we?" he asked Boslow as they left.

"Yes, sir. It's with the passenger list on the bridge."

*   *   *

Alone with Collin, Dr. Gordon pursued his reaction to the name Marshall.

"This old boss of yours, Mr. Collin, is filling his former position by any chance the promotion all you Silvers people are salivating over?"

"Yep. He was Senior VP reporting directly to Mel Silvers, and a really good guy. They shouldn't have let him leave in spite of all of us wanting that job."

"If it's the same gentleman, is it possible he was invited on this cruise without you or your associates knowing about it?"

"Are you kidding, Doctor? No way… unless…"

"Yes?"

"Nothing."

Not willing to give up this area of inquiry, Dr. Gordon persisted. "So why did Mr. Marshall leave?"

"The witch fired him. Yvonne somehow heard that he was being lured away from Silvers to run Beauty Corp., but he wasn't really pursuing it. That's how it is in our industry; competitors are always trying to pirate top talent, and Herb was very capable. Yvonne accused him of going behind her back looking for an opportunity to ransom a bigger salary. He tried to convince her that wasn't the case, but she didn't believe him and told him to pack up his desk and get out that very morning. Mel was furious with her for firing Herb, especially with our big new product launch coming up. He was even more upset when she decided to withhold Herb's bonus as well."

"Nice lady." No wonder she got her head bashed in.

"You all must have been shocked." She was fanning the embers of what sounded to her like a lot of dirty office politics.

"More outraged than shocked. We really loved working for Herb. Except for a small sales plan disagreement about a year ago, I really had no problems with him. He was the perfect manager for a group such as ours."

"I'm sure disagreements happen in every organization."

"Oh sure, but it was just a petty clash of egos. In the cosmetics business, that's the way of life."

"So in addition to the rest of you, Herb Marshall also had cause to hate Mrs. Silvers."

"Oh, even more cause after being fired the way he was, Doctor. And in addition to her nephew suing her, Herb had started litigation, too. His year-end bonus, which she refused to pay, was over 150,000 bucks."

Dr. Gordon had heard enough. If in fact the missing man was the same Herb Marshall, he may have slipped on board in San Juan for the purpose of killing Yvonne Silvers and then left the ship in Aruba. Like in so many crime investigations, this turn of events could cast a spotlight on the path of the killer. Luck and coincidence. It never fails, she thought.

"Tell you what, Mr. Collin, there's no telling how long the captain will be, so why don't we continue later? Mr. Wills will locate you when we're ready to start again."

"Suits me, Doctor. You will let me know about this Herb Marshall character that you lost, won't you? I think it's quite unlikely that it's our Herb, though."

"Thanks for your help, Mr. Collin. We'll check with you and the others later."

Dr. Gordon left a few minutes after Bill Collin. Taco was waiting for her on the railing just outside.

"Hello, Doc," Taco greeted her.

"Okay, Taco, climb aboard." She held out her forearm. "We're heading for the bridge."

"Heading for the bridge," Taco repeated.

CHAPTER 50

The Bridge

First Mate Wills was unconsciously twisting his mustache while he, Purser Boslow and Capt. Markem studied the passenger manifest. When Dr. Gordon entered the bridge, Capt. Markem looked up and addressed her. "Gwen, have a look at this," he said.

As she stepped closer to see what he was referring to, Taco hopped from her forearm onto the back of a tall stool next to one of the helmsmen who greeted the bird, "Hey, Taco, you really get around, don't you?"

"Really get around." He tilted his head back and forth as though he was part of their conversation and was hanging onto every word.

"Here's the booking information for the missing Mr. Marshall." Markem handed her the open page.

"According to this, his ticket was purchased in New York," she commented as she scanned the document.

"Yes. And as you can see, he was only booked from San Juan to Aruba," Markem pointed out.

"That's weird," Wills said. "I mean, who ever takes an overnight cruise?"

"Could be someone who wanted to get at Mrs. Silvers," Dr. Gordon suggested as she placed the manifest on a side table.

"You know," Boslow exclaimed, "I remember the man now. He came onboard that morning with the six insurance passengers."

"Can you recall anything about him, Ken?' The doctor inquired.

"Yeah, come to think of it, he was an odd-looking chap, kept his jacket collar up, as warm as it was. And I remember he was wearing heavy glasses and had a beard, a short reddish beard."

Suddenly Taco's squawk got their attention, "Red beard. All aboard."

"I'll be darned," Wills declared. "The way Taco gets around, I'll bet he saw Marshall somewhere on board."

"Jamie and I think he may have even seen the murder, and possibly the murderer," Dr. Gordon told them.

"Funny man. All aboard."

"Too bad this Marshall's not on board now," Markem lamented.

Wills and Boslow shook their heads in agreement.

"This whole thing now seems to be pointing to him, John. From what I learned from Mr. Collin, this fellow Marshall had as much reason to kill Mrs. Silvers as any of the rest of them, maybe more. She apparently threw him out of the company in a fit of rage and then cheated him out of over $150,000 in bonuses."

"Sweet lady," Boslow commented.

"Sweet lady," Taco repeated.

"Taco…" Dr. Gordon scolded as she turned toward the stool and stroked his back. "Hush now."

"Hush now. Awk."

"The fact that the passenger named Marshall had been on board that night and had then jumped ship certainly makes him a prime suspect, wouldn't you say, Gwen?"

She could see that Markem was relieved that they might have identified the killer, and was anxious to believe that the missing Marshall and the killer were one and the same person. "It certainly looks that way, Captain; however, we've yet to ID him as the Marshall who worked at Silvers." By his sudden change of expression, she knew she had just reduced his hopes a bit.

"The best way to solve that is to get Mr. Silvers in here and fast," Wills asserted.

"Then what?" Markem queried.

"If Mr. Silvers identifies him, then we contact the Aruba authorities to locate and hold him if he's still in their jurisdiction," Dr. Gordon explained.

"How do we do that?" Boslow asked.

"Through their passport control. He couldn't have gotten into Aruba without one."

"I think we should conduct the rest of this business in my quarters," Markem suggested. "The bridge is no place for this sort of thing."

"I'll have Mr. Silvers there as soon as I can locate him, Captain." Wills replaced his cap as he prepared to search for Mel.

"Just one thing," Dr. Gordon cautioned, "I'm sure Mr. Collin must have mentioned Marshall to the others, so if you're asked, just say we're checking it out and will resume our questioning shortly. I still want to keep them on edge."

"Gotcha, Gwen."

"Gotcha Gwen," Taco mimicked.

"Come on, you." She held out her forearm and Taco hopped aboard.

"Ken," Markem addressed the Purser, "I prefer that you stay here on the bridge while Wills and I are tied up with this mess."

"Yes, sir. Understood, Captain."

"I'll join you shortly," Gwen told them. "I'm taking Taco back to the infirmary. It's time for his lunch."

"Back to the infirmary. Time for lunch. Awk."

CHAPTER 51

The Captain's Quarters

When Dr. Gordon arrived, Mel was in the midst of disputing the fact that the Herb Marshall who had worked for him could have killed Yvonne.

Like her two shipmates, Markem and Wills, Dr. Gordon's hopes for an easy solution dropped like the ship's anchor, as she listened to Mel reiterate Herb's gentle qualities. "He just doesn't have that sort of violence in him, I tell you."

"We know for a fact that your wife fired him under cruel and unreasonable circumstances, Mr. Silvers." Dr. Gordon wanted him to know that they were aware of Marshall's sudden dismissal. "We also know that he was furious about her treatment of him and, on top of that, she was withholding the bonus he was due. That's more than enough motive for murder, wouldn't you agree?"

"No, I wouldn't. Not for the Herb I know."

"Are you certain, Mr. Silvers? I mean, he is listed on the ship's registry as Herb Marshall. And, according to Mr. Collin, such a person worked for you," Wills persisted.

"Bill's right about that. Herb did work for me, but it can't be the same man," Mel insisted.

"You must admit, Mr. Silvers, it's one heck of a coincidence." Then facing him directly, Dr. Gordon went on, "Please describe Mr. Marshall for me."

"I'm not very good at that sort of thing." Mel shook his head in frustration.

"Try, Mr. Silvers," Markem insisted.

"Herb's a bit younger than me, mid-fifties, not very athletic-looking. I tried to convince him to join me at the club once in a while, but he never did. He has an easy way with people and is the best marketing man I know…"

"Skip the personalities please, Mr. Silvers." Dr. Gordon was trying to be patient.

"Yes, well, he's about five ten with receding red hair and a beard that he always joked proved he could still grow hair. I can't tell you what color his eyes are because those horn-rimmed glasses he wore detracted from them… I kept telling him those glasses weren't in fashion…"

"Yes, thank you, Mr. Silvers," the doctor interrupted. For someone who can't give descriptions, you get an A-plus. She could see the expression of verification on Markem's and Will's faces when Mel mentioned the red beard and glasses.

"Still, it's quite strange," Markem addressed Mel, "that a man named Herb Marshall sneaked off the ship after your wife had been murdered. Wouldn't you agree?"

"Especially considering the circumstances by which he left your employ," Wills quickly added. "I mean, if ever anyone had a motive, this Marshall surely did."

"I suppose, but you haven't convinced me that Herb is your man. This is just too crazy," he exclaimed.

"Not at all, Mr. Silvers," Dr. Gordon persisted. "The Herb Marshall who boarded in San Juan had a red beard and wore thick glasses. Earlier your nephew told us that he thinks he saw a man with a beard near the scene of the crime. The coincidences are piling up, Mr. Silvers."

After several facial contortions and nodding his head, Mel looked back at Dr. Gordon, "I still don't believe it. It just can't be. I'm sure all of this must be a coincidence."

"Sometimes coincidences lead to the truth, Mr. Silvers."

"So am I to assume that, except for this mysterious Mr. Marshall, you haven't learned a thing from the others?"

"Not yet," Dr. Gordon disclosed. "We had only spoken to three of your associates before this Marshall business interrupted us."

"We still have a day-and-a-half before we reach port, however," Wills interjected.

"We're as anxious as you are to resolve this, Mr. Silvers." Markem's tone was sincere.

Seeing that Mel was becoming emotionally drained over the death of his wife and the fact that Herb Marshall may have killed her, Dr. Gordon concluded by stating, "We'll keep you posted, Mr. Silvers."

"Yes, fine, do that." He turned and left walking slowly and slightly bent over from the shock and trauma of it all.

*   *   *

As soon as Mel was gone, Dr. Gordon expounded on her theory. "It seems obvious that this Marshall character could be our man. I'm banking on how Mr. Silvers suddenly seemed uncertain when we laid out the facts for him."

"I agree with Gwen," Wills added. "The more I think about it, the more I'm convinced he's our man."

"We've got less than forty-eight hours to untangle this mess," Markem sighed. "What do you propose, Gwen?"

"Like I said, we should contact Aruba passport control and see if they can locate Marshall. If they do, then on your authority, Captain, and with the influence of our company's legal department, they extradite Marshall to Florida law enforcement. We'll have to release Mrs. Silvers' body to them regardless."

"I'll get on that right away, John," Wills declared.

"Just who do they look for?" Markem wondered. "A man with a red beard is rather vague."

"Describe the Herb Marshall that Silvers described, Wills - his age, thick glasses, physically out of shape," Dr. Gordon instructed. "If it's their Herb Marshall, he'd have to be carrying his official passport with his photo and address. It's pretty clever really, slip on board, kill her, then leave the ship and disappear."

"You're right, Gwen. I'll contact them right away." Wills took off immediately for the communications room to make a ship-to-shore phone call.

CHAPTER 52

The Lido Pool Buffet

The mid-day heat hit Mel as soon as he left the cool of Markem's office. After a few steps, he stopped, unbuttoned his shirt and leaned over resting his elbows on a section of the railing. The blue-green water was calm and tranquil as he stared out over it trying to compose himself. All the questioning had been an extremely distressing experience. He now had time to contemplate how such a dreadful thing could happen and alter his life so suddenly.

Although he had never admitted it to her, Yvonne had been the essence of Silvers. In spite of the horrible way she treated everyone, and the subservient role she had placed him in, she had been the one who made it a success. He wasn't sure he could carry on without her. It had always been easier to allow her to bear the burden of competition and responsibility. Now, wondering if a man he had admired and trusted had killed his wife, his remorse and fear were amplified. Somehow, he had to gather enough determination to hold everything together, not just for himself, but also for the sake of all the others, and for the memory of Yvonne. Massaging his stiff shoulders in an attempt to loosen his tight neck, he stood upright, buttoned his shirt and proceeded toward the pool area.

*   *   *

All of the group, including his nephew, Stuart, were having lunch together when Mel rejoined them.

Anxious to know why he had been called back before the remainder of them had been questioned, Barry Miller was the first to inquire. "What's going on, Mel? Bill told us that they're looking for another missing passenger and that it might be Herb."

"Isn't he the one that Aunt Yvonne tossed out and who's now suing Silvers?" Stuart was quick to ask.

"Oh boy, that does shed a whole new light on things," Simon added.

Mel could see the relief they were suddenly exhibiting on hearing that the murderer may not have been one of them, but was possibly Herb. He promptly brought them back to reality. "Before you make too much of this," he said, "it's not Herb. They thought it might be, but it's just some poor sap with a red beard and the same name."

"That's some coincidence," George Porter commented.

"Are you positive, Mel?" Jean Dawson asked with a puzzled expression.

"Jeez, people, you all worked with Herb as closely as I did. Of course, I'm sure, except..."

"Except what?" Simon and George reacted simultaneously.

"They insisted that I consider, given the circumstances of his leaving, that he had ample motive. They were pressuring me, so I might have said maybe, but it couldn't be Herb, he wouldn't harm anyone."

"That's for sure," Simon agreed.

"Then it is only a coincidence," Stuart declared.

"Yes, and coincidence or not, they'll be resuming their questioning shortly from what I gathered." Mel ordered a stiff drink.

CHAPTER 52

The Royal Palm Dining Room

The insurance company executives who boarded in San Juan were guests at the Captain's Table that evening. From their joyous, holiday nature, Dr. Gordon was pleased to see that they had no idea of the problems she and Capt. Markem were burdened with. Word of Yvonne's murder and of passengers missing and reappearing had not been divulged so far by anyone. For these celebrating passengers, the cruise was as it should be - an enjoyable and relaxing experience. Markem dutifully and politely exchanged small talk and occasionally glanced across the table toward Dr. Gordon, Nurse Brewer and Boslow.

Just by Markem's wistful expression, Dr. Gordon knew they had to solve this mess before they reached port or all of these carefree individuals would be extremely unhappy about being detained by the Fort Lauderdale authorities. The news of a prominent woman like Yvonne Silvers being murdered on board certainly wouldn't help current passenger safety concerns that were already a problem within the cruise industry.

Spotting Wills walking quickly toward the table, Dr. Gordon aimed a reassuring smile at Markem.

After courteously greeting the captain's dinner guests by name, Wills took the empty seat next to Boslow.

"Everything all right on the bridge, Mr. Wills?" Markem's question sounded official.

Dr. Gordon waited for a reassuring sign from Wills in response to Markem.

"Fine, Captain." Wills casually forked a piece of lettuce from his salad plate. "However, sir, we will need to discuss a course adjustment after dinner."

"Thank you, Mr. Wills."

Then the middle-aged gentleman to Markem's left said to him, "I do a little weekend sailing, Captain, but I guess there's a lot more involved in navigating a ship this size."

"Just a bit," Markem replied cheerfully.

Knowing all too well that under normal conditions Markem would have loved to discuss the inner working of his ship, Dr. Gordon sensed that he was now as anxious as she was to hear what Wills had learned from his phone call to Aruba. She had a feeling this dinner party would be over more quickly than usual.

Forty minutes later, after thanking his guests, Markem headed straight for his quarters with Dr. Gordon and Wills close behind.

*   *   *

"I can't remember ever having used this office as many times in one day as we have today," Markem commented.

Barely nodding her agreement, Dr. Gordon turned directly to Wills. "How did it go with the call to Aruba, Roger?"

"You're not going to believe this," he started, "my Spanish isn't the greatest and when I finally got through, the custom official's English wasn't much better…"

"Get on with it, Roger," Markem insisted anxiously.

"It's a good thing I started by telling him that we were concerned about a passenger who may have missed the boat."

"Good point, Roger," Dr. Gordon broke in briefly.

"He put me on hold while he checked his records for the day we were in port. When he came back on, he read verbatim their list of our passengers who passed through Customs that morning. Except for Marshall, they matched exactly the list of names I had for those who had re-boarded that afternoon."

"That makes no sense, Roger." Markem undid his formal bow tie, then leaned forward in frustration. "What about Herb Marshall?"

"Are you ready for this?" He tilted his head toward them. "They have no record of anyone by that name entering or leaving Aruba."

Dr. Gordon remained silent for a moment as she pondered the situation.

"Did you hear that, Gwen?" Markem ran his fingers through his thinning gray hair.

"Yes, John." Then she said to Wills, "I assume you said nothing further that would cause an international stir, Roger."

"Oh, my gosh," Markem exclaimed before Wills could respond.

"Not a word, Gwen, simply that sometimes we miscount and that I would double- check. The customs agent seemed totally uninterested in our lack of accuracy regarding loose passengers."

"Very well done, Roger." Markem breathed a sigh of relief.

"Okay, so what do we have, gentlemen?" Dr. Gordon seemed to ponder her own question for a moment. "A nasty woman who has been murdered, a prime suspect by the name of Herb Marshall who we thought had jumped ship..."

"That's it," Markem shouted, "he obviously slipped back on board and is hiding somewhere on the ship."

"We can conduct an inch by inch search, sir." Wills echoed the captain's enthusiasm. "If he's here, we'll find him."

"That's one explanation," Gwen ignored their eagerness to accept the obvious answer. "But doesn't it seem odd that he would remain on board given the opportunity he had to leave the ship in Aruba? It's more likely that he got through Aruba with a fake passport."

"What are you saying, Gwen, that we shouldn't search the ship?" Markem sounded confused.

"Yes, of course you should, and I suggest it be done discreetly," she advised.

"We can pretend we're looking for something else," Wills offered.

"Yes, but what?" Markem looked toward both of them.

"How about a certain bird that wanders all over the ship?" she replied.

"Taco. That's perfect, Gwen." Wills smiled. "Can you keep him under wraps for a few hours while we conduct our hunt?"

"No problem. Jamie and I will keep him closed up in the infirmary. As a matter of fact, while you two plan and conduct your search, I need some time on my own to study and further analyze this whole thing."

"Fine, Gwen, fine," Markem agreed as he went to a cabinet and took out a large folder.

While Markem and Wills were busy studying the deck plans of the entire ship, they never noticed her leaving.

CHAPTER 54

The Infirmary

Taco was on his perch munching on broken taco chips that Jamie had placed in his feeding cup when Dr. Gordon entered her office. "I see our little friend is living up to the name we gave him," she commented as she closed the outer door behind her.

"He really loves them," Jamie replied. "The entire kitchen staff knows it and they make sure he has a steady supply. They just sent down another bagfull they had collected from snack trays on the bars."

Plopping into her desk chair, Dr. Gordon explained what had transpired so far, including the search for Mr. Marshall and the pretext that it was being conducted to find Taco.

"I wondered why you shut the outer door. So what happens if they don't find him?" Jamie settled on the corner of the doctor's desk.

"I don't think they will, but I don't know why. If only our chip-loving friend over there could talk." They both laughed knowing the bird was a chatterbox. "You know what I mean, Jamie." They chuckled again. "I'm convinced that he saw Mrs. Silvers being bludgeoned…"

Taco appeared to sense that they were talking about him. He tilted his head to one side and repeated, "Bludgeoned. Bad lady."

"He was there, weren't you, Taco? Did you see the bad lady fall?" Jamie coaxed him.

"Putting the words in his beak won't prove a thing," Dr. Gordon chided. "In the meantime, I've got a little checking to do on my own. Keep Taco in here with you. I'll be back in a while."

"No problem. He's content at the moment and I'm almost through a Robert's love story." She picked up a well-worn paperback, one of many that were being circulated around the ship by various crewmembers.

"Enjoy your book," Dr. Gordon said as she left the infirmary.

*   *   *

Her first stop was to visit Mel Silvers. She finally located him having a drink in the small bar off the Lido Pool buffet area a good distance away from the rest of the group who were still gathered around the pool. He appeared tired and a bit disheveled, obviously deeply affected by the loss of his wife in spite of her cruel behavior. He also appeared to be suffering from lack of sleep.

"I'm sorry to intrude, Mr. Silvers, but I need your help with something. May I join you for a moment?"

A bit startled, he put his glass down and started to rise, an automatic gesture by an obvious gentleman. "Of course, Doctor..."

She placed her hand on his shoulder. "Please stay seated."

He sank back into the soft, cushioned lounge chair. "Any new developments, Doctor?"

"Nothing that I can be certain of at the moment, I'm afraid."

He picked up his drink. "Can I order you something?"

"No, thanks."

He took a sip. "You said you needed my help?"

She explained what she was looking for, after which he took out his pen and scribbled on a cocktail napkin. Handing the makeshift note to her, he asked, "Can you tell me why you need this information?"

"Just as soon as I'm certain of what it is I'm looking for, Mr. Silvers."

"Suit yourself, Doctor." He took a large drink and drained the glass.

Pocketing the napkin, Gwen rose and thanked him. As she left, he ordered another drink, and she had to wonder whether he was truly grief-stricken or was he celebrating.

CHAPTER 55

Communications Room

"Hey, Doc, any luck finding Taco?" Bert Thomas, the ship's radio and phone operator, greeted Dr. Gordon when she entered his domain of microphones, headphones and other types of computerized communications equipment.

"Not yet, Bert, but you know Taco, he's probably off in some corner of the ship jabbering with an amused passenger."

"That's what I told Mr. Wills when he came by here earlier."

Gwen Gordon liked Bert. He was far from the stereotypical radio engineer she had seen in a number of ocean-going B-movies. Bert had an intelligent look about him and his junior college education backed it up. Like her, he found sea life more rewarding than operating a small midwestern TV control panel.

He put aside a paperback he had been reading when she came in. "This novel you loaned me, Doc, I'm reading it, but I'm afraid I'm not into Higgins."

"She's not for everyone, Bert."

The size of the communications room was in keeping with the scale of the Coral Queen, small but very functional. Dr. Gordon, however, found it too tight for her comfort, so she got right to the reason for her visit.

"I need an open phone line to New York, Bert."

"You got it, Doc." He pushed a few buttons, then turned and pointed to a phone on a small table near him.

After dialing the number she read from the cocktail napkin, she waited until she heard, "Silvers Cosmetics, how may I direct your call?"

"Extension 213," Dr. Gordon requested.

"This is Nora Coleman."

"Hello, Ms. Coleman. My name is Gwen Gordon. I'm the assistant purser on the Coral Queen, out of Fort Lauderdale. I understand you handle the travel arrangements for Silvers executives."

"That's correct, Ms. Gordon, and how may I help you?" came the cheery reply.

"As you are no doubt aware, we are currently hosting a number of your people on our select five-day Caribbean cruise…"

"That's correct. Is there a problem?" Ms. Cheery went to Ms. Concerned.

"Oh no, just a discrepancy in the reservations that I would like to clear up before the charges go to our accounting department."

"Like what?" Ms. Concerned now became Ms. Challenged. "I'm sure we booked properly from our end."

"Oh, no, Ms. Coleman, it's nothing like that." Dr. Gordon's tone was so apologetic that she could see the confused look on Bert's face over what was transpiring. She cupped the phone and whispered to him,"I'll explain later."

He shrugged his shoulders, leaned back and listened.

"It's just that," Dr. Gordon continued with Coleman, "we have one of your VPs listed on our manifest, but he doesn't appear to be on board."

"Oh, my heavens." Ms. Challenged now went back to Ms. Very Concerned. "Who's missing? Oh boy, I'll bet Mrs. Silvers is furious." Her voiced cracked.

She's far from furious now, Dr. Gordon thought. "It's a gentleman by the name of Herb Marshall. I believe he's your Executive VP." Knowing he was no longer with the company, Dr. Gordon fired his name at Coleman mostly for a reaction. And she got one as fast as Coleman could deliver it.

"You're mistaken, Ms. Gordon." Ms. Very Concerned switched to Ms. Very Relieved. "Mr. Marshall is no longer with us and I certainly didn't book him for your cruise."

"I see." Dr. Gordon wasn't getting exactly what she had called for, but it was information, nonetheless. "And you're the only one in your company who would handle such arrangements?"

"Yes, of course. I do hope this will not prevent my superiors from enjoying their trip, Ms. Gordon."

"Oh no, rest assured the champagne is flowing and they're being well attended to," she replied facetiously.

"I'm glad to hear that." Ms. Coleman was Ms. Cheery again.

"Thank you, Ms. Coleman. It's obviously a glitch in our booking system."

"Obviously." Ms. Cheery became Ms. Impeccable, then hung up.

After placing the phone down and before he could ask, Dr. Gordon turned to Bert and said, "It's kind of complicated, Bert, and it's something the Captain wants kept confidential. Got it?"

"I know about the dead lady, Doc."

"All the more reason to keep a zipped lip, Bert."

"Gotcha." He made a lip-zipping gesture.

"Now I need to place another call." She referred to the cocktail napkin again.

CHAPTER 56

The Infirmary

"He's been quite restless since he can't go wandering about," Jamie told Dr. Gordon when she finally returned from Bert's communications room.

"Taco restless." He paced back and forth on his perch.

"Not just yet, my feathered friend." Dr. Gordon stroked his yellow head. Then turning her attention back to Jamie, she said, "We'll let him out as soon as I hear from Wills or the Captain. They should be through with their mock search before too long."

"It can't be too soon for either of us," Jamie declared. "I think he's as bored as I am. He's been clawing and fussing around in his private little storage area on top of that upper file cabinet for almost an hour."

"Who knows what shiny little treasures he's got up there." Dr. Gordon stretched up onto her toes but couldn't see over the top. "It's due for a good cleaning soon."

"Cleaning soon." He flew the short distance from his perch back up onto the tall cabinet. All they could see was his tail flicking in their direction while he rummaged through his things, tossing them here and there, apparently rearranging his cache.

"And what have you been up to this past hour, Dr. G?" Jamie asked ignoring Taco's activity on the top of the cabinet.

Dr. Gordon explained the calls she had made earlier and the conclusions she had drawn from what she had discovered. "It's nothing to pin a murder on yet, but it sure points us in the right direction," she confided to her nurse.

It was only a few minutes later when Wills called. "Gwen," he said, "we've completed the search and it was fruitless. I saw corners of the ship that I didn't know existed. Captain wants to know what's left to do other than wait until we reach port. He's really frustrated."

"Tell him to hang tight. I've got a good idea what the answer to all this is, but I don't have enough positive proof yet." She could hear Wills relaying the message to Capt. Markem.

"Captain says come to his quarters, Gwen. He's willing to listen to anything at this point."

"Be there shortly."

"Can I let this restless creature out now?" Jamie asked.

"Sure, I'll leave the door open behind me. Pour some more chips in his cup. That will calm him down and then he'll go find someone else to visit with," Dr. Gordon suggested as she rushed out.

Jamie dumped the treats into Taco's cup and headed for the crew's cafeteria.

CHAPTER 57

The Captain's Quarters

Wills and Markem were having a bite of lunch when Dr. Gordon showed up.

"We thought you were coming directly here, Gwen." Markem wiped his mouth. "We ordered sandwiches and tea for you."

"Thanks, I'd almost forgotten I was hungry." She joined them at the table and reached for half a ham and cheese.

"I hope the tea is still warm." Wills touched the side of the china pot.

"I'm sure it's fine. I had to make a quick stop on my way," she explained as Markem poured her a cup of tea, "and, I'm glad I did."

"Wills says you may be close to resolving this mess of ours." Markem sounded hopeful.

"I took a close look at the cabin on C deck that our missing Mr. Marshall occupied," she explained between chews. After a gulp of tea, she continued, "It's a good thing we closed off that room when we thought he was the culprit..." She took another sip of tea. "Because I found what I hoped would be there." She tapped a white envelope tucked in her blouse pocket.

"For heaven sake, Gwen, are you going to explain what you're talking about?" Markem inquired anxiously.

"Come on, Gwen, what have you been up to? Time's running out," Wills reminded her.

The sudden ringing of the Captain's phone distracted them.

Answering it, Markem said, "Yes, she's here, just a minute, Jamie." He held the phone out to Dr. Gordon.

Hoping it wasn't a medical problem, she licked some mayo off her fingers and took the receiver. "Yes, Jamie?"

"I thought you should know what I found down here when I returned from lunch, Gwen."

"Oh?"

"Seems Taco did his own housecleaning from on top of the cabinet and you'll never guess what he dropped on your desk."

"Don't tell me he…"

"No, no, Dr. G, nothing like that." Jamie went on to tell her what she had found.

"That ties another knot in the rope, Jamie. It's very possible he picked it up the night of the murder."

"I'm sure of it, Gwen."

"Hang onto it. I'll need it later to prove my theory." She hung up facing dual confused looks from her two companions.

"What's happening, Gwen?" Markem asked.

For the next several minutes she told them in detail who she believed the murderer was and how she thought it had been accomplished.

When she finished, Wills was the first to respond. "That's ingenious, Gwen, but not solid enough to place the killer in irons till we get to port."

"Is what she says possible, Wills?" Markem questioned his First Mate.

"The way she explains it, it is, John," Wills conceded.

"It's a diabolical scheme all right, but all of your evidence so far seems to be circumstantial. I'm not sure we can make it stick," Markem exclaimed.

"There's only one way," she announced. "I saw enough of the technique in Jersey to enable me to put it into play. All

I'll need is for you two to go along with whatever I say and do. Now, Wills, just like every Sherlock movie you've ever seen, let's gather all the suspects into the ship's library and see what develops."

CHAPTER 58

The Ship's Library

Like most reading rooms, the ship's library, though small, had been designed with reading comfort in mind. One wall of the thirty by thirty foot space was floor to ceiling oak shelving filled with an array of hardcover books from current titles to many of the old classics. On the opposite wall stood a magazine rack with the latest issues available when the ship left port four days earlier. Dark paneling, thick carpeting and a dozen or so cozy chairs strategically placed contributed to the sound-absorbing ambiance of the library.

Except for Mel and the Dumonts, Wills had gathered the remainder of the Silvers group and they were assembled there. The Captain, Dr. Gordon and Jamie Brewer, with Taco on her arm, had just joined them.

Moving to the magazine rack, Jamie deposited the bird on one of the holding rods. "You behave now," she whispered.

"Behave now." He imitated her hushed voice and looked around the room.

Harriet Porter was the first to speak. "I strongly protest the horrible situation we've all been placed in as a result of Yvonne's demise," she complained. "And I must add that I personally have been under considerable stress since the beginning of this cruise."

"You should have let me know, Mrs. Porter, I could have given you something to relax you," Dr. Gordon replied.

"Drugs are not the answer to everything, Doctor." Harriet turned away in a huff.

"She's right, you know, Captain." Jean Dawson lent her support to Harriet.

"And would you please explain why exactly we've been corralled here now."

She's acting true to form, Dr. Gordon thought as Jean Dawson addressed the male member of their trio.

"I'm sure the Captain and Doctor know what they're doing, Jean." Jim Dawson tried to calm his wife.

"We'll try to explain everything as soon as the rest of your group arrives." Markem's reply was intended for all of them. "Meanwhile, please make yourselves comfortable and, if you like, we can order some refreshments."

"This is hardly the time to think of drinks, Captain," Stuart Rosen, seated cross-legged in a suede chair, commented and snidely added, "especially since we still don't know who killed my aunt."

"Perhaps that's what this is all about, Stuart," Barry Miller retorted.

Stuart switched knees. "I hope so."

"You know, Mr. Rosen, shoe marks are difficult to remove from suede," Marge Collin observed.

Her husband, Bill, merely shook his head knowing she would never change.

"Oh, for heaven sakes, Marge," Helen Miller snapped. "Who gives a darn about that chair? We all just want to get home."

"Calm down, all of you. I'm sure the Captain and Dr. Gordon have their reasons for calling us all together like this," George Porter advised.

Dr. Gordon listened and waited.

Wills's entry with the Dumonts momentarily broke the tension. "Mr. Silvers will be along in a minute," he announced.

"This looks like a gathering on the Titanic," Simon joked.

"I don't think this is the time for your warped sense of humor." His wife, Dina, elbowed him.

Mel Silvers arrived, greeted his staff, and took a seat near his nephew.

"Good, now that you are all here, we can proceed. Dr. Gordon, if you will." Captain Markem verbally gave her the floor.

"We know you've all had a very difficult few days since the loss of Mrs. Silvers and with all the questioning and probing that followed. Needless to say, it has not been the cruise you anticipated when you boarded four days ago in Fort Lauderdale, nor is it the cruise we normally provide to our esteemed passengers…"

"Humph." Harriet Porter's negative vocalization was loud enough to interrupt Dr. Gordon.

"And for that we are sorry." Dr. Gordon ignored the woman's sarcasm. "However, murder is a nasty bit of business, especially for the innocent who come under suspicion. That is, except for one of you. Had it not been for a number of things that came to my attention, this gathering of all of you, along with the other passengers on board, would be taking place at the Fort Lauderdale Police Headquarters tomorrow, and believe me, it would be a much more grueling and lengthy experience for all concerned."

"Are you telling us, Doctor, that you know who murdered Yvonne?" Mel Silvers stood up abruptly and faced her.

"Yes, I am, Mr. Silvers, but I must say it's a rather convoluted set of circumstances. First, there's the fact that every one of you had reason to hate the late Mrs. Silvers and that didn't help matters. I understand, for example, that in spite of Mr. Dumont's lack of interest in the promotion, her treatment of him was belittling enough so that I'm sure he won't miss her at all."

"That's uncalled for, Dr. Gordon. My Simon is a sensitive artist," Dina shrieked. "It's true she treated him like dirt, but not nearly as much as what she put her own husband, Mel, through."

"Now Dina, there's no point in bringing that up now," Mel admonished.

"Come on, Mel, she's right, and you know it. Yvonne never let up on you. She was always insinuating that Jean was your favorite and that you shored up her merchandising efforts," Barry spouted.

Dr. Gordon allowed them to squabble. "Is that true, Mr. Silvers?" She fanned the coals of the corporate inferno.

"No, it's not," Jean Dawson stated indignantly. "If anything, Mel supported you, Barry, every time Yvonne insisted that you were only half the marketing man Herb was. And what about, Bill?" she continued. "He could hardly contain himself whenever Yvonne cut his department's sales commissions to make up for a weak bottom line. He had every reason to hate her."

"No more so than George," Bill Collin piped in. "R&D was a joke as far as Yvonne was concerned. She never supported half of his needs."

"What a cast of suspects," Stuart finally spoke up mocking the entire scenario. "Seems like you all wanted my poor aunt dead."

"Oh, I don't know about that, Mr. Rosen. There's some pretty damning evidence against you as well." Dr. Gordon held up a slip of paper.

"And what might that be, Doctor?"

"Just a note that one of the cleaning crew found on deck the morning after the murder." She proceeded to read it to him. "Sorry Auntie, I would only work there over your dead body." She folded it and handed it to Markem.

"Oh no, Stuart, how could you?" Mel Silvers shouted to his nephew. "It wasn't worth it."

"Well there you have it," Dr. Gordon addressed her baffled audience. "I perceived a ripe potential in each of you and even more so with Stuart here, until…" then she paused, "until I discovered a very clever and deceptive plan that developed before you left New York. If it hadn't started there, we might never have known that it was George Porter who killed Yvonne Silvers."

"What? Are you insane, Doctor? My husband wasn't even on board when Yvonne was murdered," Harriet Porter screamed.

"This must be some sort of joke," George said calmly as he chewed on a dry pipe.

"Far from it, Mr. Porter."

"We understood that Herb Marshall was under suspicion," Jean Dawson exclaimed.

"Yeah, how about him?" Barry Miller asked. "Mel told us he wasn't sure it was Herb at first when you described the man with the red beard. But then, when he disappeared in Aruba, well... we all began to wonder..."

"Like I said," Dr. Gordon quickly continued, "it was an ingenious plan on Mr. Porter's part."

"This is stupid," George Porter snapped. "If you allow her to continue with this false accusation, Capt. Markem, this cruise line is subject to one large lawsuit."

"Not to mention the mental anguish I endured when you left my husband behind in San Juan," Harriet reiterated.

"I'm sorry, Mrs. Porter, but I'm afraid you're in for considerably more anguish," Dr. Gordon went on. "After I spoke with Ms. Coleman, the travel specialist for Silvers, I learned that Mr. Marshall was never booked for this cruise since he had already left the company."

"That doesn't prove very much, Doctor," Bill Collin argued.

"Of course it doesn't, Mr. Collin," she continued. "That's why I requested Mr. Marshall's home number. As I was able to speak to him at his home in Westchester, it should be obvious to all of you that he never left New York. And here's where the clever part comes in, Mr. Porter." Dr. Gordon moved in his direction as she spoke and as she did so all eyes focused on the two of them. "Your first mistake was to involve Marshall in the first place. After speaking to Ms. Coleman and Mr. Marshall, my third phone call was to our booking department in Fort Lauderdale. Their records show that Mr. Marshall's booking was paid for in cash through a New York travel agency."

"What does that prove, Captain?" Harriet shouted. "Anyone could have done that."

"Please, Mrs. Porter, allow Dr. Gordon to continue."

"Yes, be quiet, Harriet, I'd like to hear more myself," Mel insisted.

Dr. Gordon studied her suspect as she went on. Porter wasn't displaying any signs of guilt yet, but she felt certain he would with her next volley of facts. And when he did, she would lay on some fiction that would hopefully do him in. "Of course your wife is correct, isn't she, Mr. Porter? Any one of you could have purchased that booking."

"You're fishing now, Doctor," he replied smugly.

"Am I? That booking was paid for from San Juan to Aruba. And since Herb Marshall never left New York, who boarded in his place wearing a red beard and horn-rimmed glasses? It could only have been you, Mr. Porter, who came back on board in disguise and then hid out in the room on C deck reserved for Mr. Marshall."

"Sorry, Doctor, you've got the wrong red-bearded man." He still showed no signs of cracking.

In silent awe everyone else watched what was transpiring between the two of them.

"You forget, Dr. Gordon, that I called my wife when I missed the boat."

"That's right, Doctor, did you forget about that?" Harriet burst in.

"Not at all." Dr. Gordon picked up from there. "You see, when I was in our communications room making those phone calls, I also had our radio operator check his computer log for ship-to-shore calls that day, and there were none. The call you thought was coming from shore, Mrs. Porter, was in fact coming from cabin 6C, the room reserved for Mr. Marshall."

"George! What in heaven's name is she talking about?" Harriet snapped.

"It doesn't prove it was me, Harriet. This is simply nonsense. We all know computers louse up all the time." He seemed to be clenching his teeth a little tighter on his pipe stem.

"In your disguise, you followed Mrs. Silvers and her nephew after they left the Royal Palms Dining Room together." Dr. Gordon was standing next to Porter now. Wills also stood close at hand. "Then you waited in the shadows outside of the Fifties Lounge until Mrs. Silvers came out alone. You followed her and, further down the deck, you bludgeoned her with the complimentary champagne bottle from cabin 6C."

"All speculation and no witnesses, Doctor. The longer you continue these false accusations before this entire room of witnesses, the bigger my defamation suit will be."

"Oh, we do have a witness, Mr. Porter." She watched closely as it hit him. His eyes twitched ever so slightly, but she caught it. "It seems our little busy-body, Taco, was perched nearby when you tossed Mrs. Silvers over the side."

"A bird? That dumb parrot is your witness?" Harriet Porter shrieked.

"Preposterous," her husband added.

"Perhaps. However, we know he was there because afterwards he kept repeating 'man overboard'."

Suddenly, from the magazine rack, Taco squawked, "Man overboard. Awk."

Ignoring the parrot, Dr. Gordon continued. "There's also this that we're sure he picked up at the scene of the crime." She removed an almost empty, gold foil tobacco pouch from her pocket. Holding it up, she read aloud, "Special blend for G.P. The Pipe Den, Fifth Ave., New York, NY."

"He could have picked that up anywhere on board. You all know he followed me everywhere."

"Precisely," Dr. Gordon said, "which is why even with that beard, we think he knew it was you who killed Mrs. Silvers." Then she added, "It's a known fact that animals and birds have a very keen sense of recognition."

"Man overboard. Hello, George," came from the magazine rack again.

"How could you have done such a thing?" Mel Silvers jumped up sobbing and yelling, "How could you?" His nephew grabbed him and guided him back to his seat.

"It's all nonsense, Mel," Porter shouted back.

This is exactly the agitation Dr. Gordon wanted. "And then, of course, there are these, Mr. Porter." She held up a couple of bent and soiled pipe cleaners.

"Another cute trick by your parrot, Doctor?"

She could see a bead of perspiration forming on his temple. "We found these in room 6C, Mr. Porter, and since you're the only pipe smoker in the group, we know you inadvertently left them. Then the morning after the murder when you disembarked in Aruba as Herb Marshall, you discarded your disguise in a nearby restroom and, without having to go through passport control, re-boarded as yourself."

"This is all well and good, Doctor, but you'll have a devil of a time convincing the police of any of this. I've had more than enough of your meddling…"

"And then, of course," she continued over his objections, "my last phone call was to Trans Islands Airways. They island hop between San Juan and Aruba and they have no record of your being on any flight."

"They're mistaken. A small airline like that can't keep very good records." He clenched his pipe bowl tightly.

"On the contrary, Mr. Porter, I think they keep very good records. However, we have something much more convincing than what I've explained so far." At this point she hoped that Markem and Wills would remember to go along with whatever she sprung on him. "You see, Mr. Porter, as soon as we suspected that Mr. Marshall had killed Mrs. Silvers and then jumped ship in Aruba, we sealed off room 6C. That's how I found your pipe cleaners and that's where the police will find your fingerprints."

"Okay, but all that proves is that I was in the room and nothing more," he replied defiantly.

"Not quite, Mr. Porter. There's also this." Dr. Gordon turned toward Jamie who in turn handed her a large, clear food storage bag containing a green champagne bottle. "It's the murder weapon," she declared. "There'll be no denying your fingerprints on it."

"How did you..." George reached for the bottle.

Wills quickly grabbed him and held him back.

"I'm afraid, Mr. Porter, rather than the murder weapon landing in the sea to be lost forever, it landed on the canvas cover of the lifeboat next to her. That pieces everything I explained together."

"But George," interjected Harriet, "you seemed genuinely shocked when they found Yvonne's body."

"I was," he replied. "She wasn't supposed to end up in that lifeboat. She was supposed to go into the ocean and disappear forever, a feast for the fishes. But she couldn't even do that without taunting me in the end. Don't you understand, Harriet? She was tormenting all of us. Nothing was ever good enough. No matter what we did, she always found fault, a reason to ridicule us, to make us feel inferior. Herb was the smart one. He escaped and, when he did, he told me that none of us would ever get his job no matter how much we wanted it or how hard we worked. He said she was going to give it to her nephew... another Rosen. And he laughed. Herb actually laughed in my face, called me a loser. That's when I decided to get both of them, Yvonne and Herb, too. I'd do her in and embroil him to the point of causing him a great deal of legal grief."

"George!" his wife screamed, "how could you be so cruel and so stupid?"

"Shut up, Harriet. It's all your fault."

This is what Gwen had hoped to work him up to.

"My fault? How dare you blame me for the death of another human being." She started to swoon, and Simon, who was the closest to her, eased her into a chair.

"You're almost as bad as she was, Harriet, constantly complaining about my not getting ahead faster and berating me for letting Herb Marshall take the credit for my efforts.

Then you drove me crazy when you heard his job was available, insisting I should push hard to get it. I practically begged Yvonne for that promotion more for peace of mind than any other reason. All she ever did was rub my nose in the dirt, telling me I wasn't as capable as Herb and never would be. That woman didn't deserve to live, and I'm not sorry I bashed her head in."

Gwen Gordon could see the signs of relief on Markem's face. They needed a confession and she had gotten it. The rest of the Silvers group slowly backed away, either dumbstruck over what George Porter had done, or silently grateful to him for doing what they all wished they could have done.

Wills and Markem stood on either side of Porter as the group slowly walked out of the library.

Mel Silvers, being supported by his nephew, Stuart, was in a state of shock. They stopped for a moment. Mel looked up at Porter and said, "You evil man, and to think you were my choice to replace Herb."

"Yeah, Mel, you wimp, at least I did something about the problem," Porter snapped as he turned his back on his would-be mentor.

During the exchange between Mel and Porter, Markem whispered to Dr. Gordon, "Why didn't you tell me you found the murder weapon, Gwen?"

"We didn't, John," she whispered back with a wink.

Wills and Markem led Porter out to lock him in an empty cabin until they reached Fort Lauderdale the next morning. As they passed the magazine rack where Taco was perched, Taco had the last word.

"Goodbye, George. Goodbye Funny man."

*   *   *

THE END